Raining Fire

ALAN GIBBONS

Read on!

Alan Gibbons

30.6.16

Indigo

First published in Great Britain in 2013
by Indigo
a division of the Orion Publishing Group Ltd
Orion House
5 Upper St Martin's Lane
London WC2H 9EA
An Hachette UK Company

1 3 5 7 9 10 8 6 4 2

A catalogue record for this book
is available from the British Library

ISBN 978 1 78062 027 5

Typeset by Input Data Services Ltd, Bridgwater, Somerset

Printed and bound by CPI Group (UK) Ltd, Croydon, CR0 4YY

www.orionbooks.co.uk

To Rhys Jones and Anuj Bidve

Author's Note

The two great cities of the North West, Manchester and Liverpool, provide the background for most of my writing. This is where I have lived and worked most of my adult life. This is where my wife and I raised our family. The North West is, as Gerry Marsden sang in Ferry 'Cross the Mersey 'the place I love.'

But there is a dark side to both cities, an undercurrent of violent crime.

Already haunted by the murder of little Jamie Bulger by two young boys, Liverpool was shaken again in 2007 when eleven-year-old Rhys Jones was killed by a gunman's bullet on his way home from football practice. Rhys was the innocent victim of gang rivalry.

On Boxing Day, 2011 Greater Manchester had its own senseless killing when Kiaran Stapleton shot dead promising student Anuj Bidve in cold blood. He has never given a reason for what he did.

Gun slayings are thankfully rare in the UK, but incidents involving firearms have become disturbingly regular events. During the riots in August 2011 shots were fired at police in Birmingham.

As a teacher and author I have spoken to a number of youngsters for whom school and academic success held little attraction. Growing up on bleak, jobless estates, they saw sport or crime as the only pathways out of poverty and boredom. Some spoke of the buzz they got from hanging round in gangs. I wanted to explore this world, neither to make judgements, nor to glamorise, but to understand.

Alan Gibbons
Liverpool
August 2012

PART ONE

BEFORE THE FIRE

The gun is power.

The gun can make a weak man strong. The gun is the coward's fist. It has no moral conscience, no will of its own. It can destroy close up or at a distance. The gunman can choose to look into the eyes of his victim or avoid the stare of the dying. The gunman doesn't have to feel the intimacy of death. The kill is the perfect remote act. It combines computer-game morality and a fatal bullet. A shot to the head. A shot to the heart. Either way the gun delivers.

Every time.

It does its job.

Every time.

I was fourteen when I met the gun. It was the first time I'd ever seen one for real. It wouldn't be the last. I would learn to love – and hate – the gun. I would struggle with its attraction and its power. I would look down the barrel and make others do the same. Everything happened in two years. Two short years from start to finish, from temptation to surrender to, well, wherever I am now.

Two years; is that all it is? When I look back it feels longer. It's a lifetime of decisions right and wrong, of sacrifice, crime and punishment. The night I met the gun I fought to get a look.

'Let me see.'

I squirmed into the group. Everybody was crowding around Jamie Leather. Mitch was shoving too. We were the youngest ones there. The gun drew us like moths to a light bulb. I kept pushing and jostling into the heart of the crowd. It was Bonfire Night. I could smell the November rain steaming on the older boys' uniform black jackets. It mixed with the cordite in the air. All eyes were on the gun.

'Is it real?'

Jamie saw me making my way forward. My question amused him. He spoke to somebody standing behind him, my brother Alex.

'Hear that? Your kid wants to know if this piece is real.'

Jamie wasn't the tallest or the most powerfully built of the group. If somebody had asked you to pick out the leader, you'd probably pass him by. He didn't go out of his way to get noticed. He didn't need to. At seventeen he was lean and wiry with broad shoulders out of proportion to the rest of his frame. He wore his hair shaved right down to the scalp, and a tattoo round the rim of his right eye. It was in the shape of a claw.

Somebody on our street once called him a hyena. He didn't say it twice, not to Jamie's face. People who fell out with Jamie Leather got hurt. It's the law of wild places. The lion is king; he's the showman of the savannah. He

4

gets all the attention. But it's the hyena that does most of the killing.

Jamie reached out a hand, wrapping his fingers round my neck. He pulled me in among the older boys. He was admitting me into the inner circle. I could feel the strength in his fingers. I tried to pull back, but there was no fighting him. His voice crackled with excitement, almost obsession. It was an incantation, a hymn to the power of the gun.

'This is my favourite weapon. It's a Walther PPK semi-automatic pistol. It shoots a .380 round.'

I became aware of Alex, my older brother. I watched him, saw the way his eyes never left the gun, saw the hunger in his gaze. My attention returned to the gun. I looked at the stainless steel finish. There was a kind of hard beauty about it.

'That's a replica,' I snorted. 'You wouldn't be waving a real one around.'

Jamie's fat, almost swollen lips curled into a smile. The eye tattoo wrinkled. 'Do you know who had one of these?' he said. 'This is the James Bond gun.' He was playing to the crowd.

Somebody laughed in my ear. 'Hear that? Jamie's got a licence to kill.'

Somebody shouted from the back. 'Bring on the girls. I've got a licence to th-r-r-r-ill.'

That set everyone off. Jamie was laughing. So was Alex. I saw Mitch. He was laughing along with everyone else, but he was on the outside. He wanted in.

'No Ethan, this isn't a replica.' Jamie was suddenly earnest. He took out the magazine. 'What we have here is a six-round magazine capable of lethal force. Take a look if you want.' For a moment the barrel lingered in front of my face. 'See that. He didn't even flinch.'

I had passed some sort of test.

'This is my boy.'

Alex was put out. He didn't like Jamie giving me all the attention.

Jamie nodded at the barrel. 'This is the last thing a man sees when he takes a bullet.'

I did my best to face the gun down. 'You mean you've been carrying a loaded weapon around with you? You're mad.'

Mad.

It's a double-edged word, mad. There's insane, then there's so brave you're crazy. That's the definition they go for on the street. Dominant male. Fearless. You're the main man.

'Can't do anything with it otherwise. No need to get scared, kid. Now the magazine's out, it can't do you any harm.'

I pulled away. Who was he calling a kid? Who was he calling scared? He and Alex might be three years older. That didn't impress me.

'Your stupid gun doesn't frighten me.'

That set off more laughter. Jamie's hand was back round my neck. It made my skin clammy. There was that discomforting strength again. He winked in Alex's direction.

'Bit of a fighting cock, your little brother.' He wrestled me around then let go. 'See the way he holds his chin up. Ethan's proud.'

I shoved at him, but he held me close.

'You're a soldier.' He jabbed at Alex's foot with the

toe of his trainer. 'You belong to the Tribe, just like Alex here.'

Being a soldier made you somebody on the Green. People shot furtive glances then hurried by. Stuff like that gave you a reputation. Somebody lit up. It illuminated our faces. We were the Green's Lost Boys, the Tribe, all scrawny, all swathed in black, all looking out from under caps or hoods, sometimes both. Every pair of eyes was on the pistol.

'Now, let's take a look at the gun. This is a blowback design.'

I caught Mitch's eye and saw his blank look. Jamie didn't explain. That was the whole point. The gun is a mystery. It has a kind of magic. Knowing the killer details marked Jamie out as the main man, the wizard. I nodded anyway. He carried on showing off.

'You can pull the trigger in a double action like this.' He showed us. 'Or you can cock the hammer like this. See, that's a single action.'

There was a shout over his shoulder. 'Same result, isn't it?' It was the boy who cracked the licence to thrill joke. Comedy Guy blew a gunshot noise into the back of his hand and staggered back clutching his chest. He wasn't getting any laughs so he slunk sheepishly back into the group.

Jamie offered me the gun. When I hesitated Alex muscled in and took it without hesitation. He held it in a two-handed grip. He planted his feet and squinted along the barrel. Then he laughed and offered it to me.

'What do you say, Ethan? Want a go?'

I kept my hands by my side. Mitch saw his chance and took it. He looked around. Comedy Guy wasn't paying attention. Mitch came up behind him and shoved the barrel of the gun under his chin. There was a bang and Mitch laughed. Comedy Guy went slack, horror blanching his face.

'That was a firework, crap for brains. It's Bonfire Night.' He slapped the boy across his head. 'You nearly wet yourself.'

Comedy Guy's cheeks burned with humiliation. Jamie seemed to notice Mitch for the first time.

'Looks like we've got another gangster here.'

More fireworks crackled round the estate. I was still watching Mitch with the gun when I heard my name.

'Ethan!'

Recognising the familiar North East burr, I turned. Not here. Not now.

'I've been looking for you.'

'Eddie. What are you doing down this way?'

Mitch no longer had the gun. I guessed Jamie had it.

'You missed training. I want to know why.'

I swallowed. Eddie's the one who scouted me, got me my chance at the Academy. People say he's one of the canniest scouts of young talent in the Premiership. Had he seen the gun? This could mean expulsion. My flesh was crawling.

'Ethan, come here, son. I want a word in your shell-like.'

One lad laughed.

'Who's the geriatric, Ethan?'

Eddie gave him the dead eye.

'Watch your mouth, rat boy.'

It was said with enough conviction to silence the kid. The rat boy might have the measure of his teachers, but he sensed Eddie's quiet authority. I flicked a glance in the direction of the weapon. I couldn't see who had it. My neck was burning. Did Eddie know? To my relief, Alex passed the piece to his left and Jamie pocketed it. Eddie drew me to one side.

'Did you forget something this evening? What was it Ethan, spontaneous amnesia?'

My heart rate steadied. Eddie hadn't seen the gun. I pulled a face.

'Give me a break, Eddie,' I said. 'So I gave training a miss. It's no big deal.'

'That right?' Eddie growled. 'I didn't know you were such an expert. Invented a new theory, have you? Success is in inverse proportion to the effort you put in.'

He stared me down. 'Let me give you a piece of advice, bonny lad: not many kids round here get the kind of chance the club has given you. You could make it, Ethan. You could sign professional forms.'

I imagined people buying their shirts from the club shop.

Number 8 on the back.

My name.

Holt.

'You could go all the way, play in the Premiership, be somebody. Think you're going to do it pulling stupid tricks like this?'

His gaze wandered round the boys assembled on the far pavement.

'Is this what you want?'

I shrugged.

'You've got your priorities wrong, son. You know where you'll end up messing with these clowns? Prison, that's the size of it.'

9

'They're my mates.'

'They're silly, little boys pretending to be men.' Eddie drummed his fingers on the dash. 'I thought you were better than this. Do you remember what you promised me?'

'I remember.'

'You told me you lived for your football. I thought I could see dedication. Was I wrong about you?'

He hammered home the point.

'I picked you out of the junior league when you were nine. You got promoted to the over-elevens, playing with lads eighteen months, two years older than you.'

'You don't need to remind me, Ed.'

'Oh, I think I do, Ethan. Talent got you this far. Talent and hard work.'

The memories came back. Eddie was my mentor, had been from the very beginning. We had a bond.

'I haven't changed, Ed. Football's everything. You know how I feel.'

'Yes? So why did you give training a miss? Does your mum know you went missing?'

He saw the answer in my face.

'No, I thought not.'

I felt a sense of injustice. I had my reasons.

'It isn't all my fault, you know. Mick's always on my back.'

The coach, Mick Laverty, was a disciplinarian. I didn't like people laying down the law.

'So that's it,' Eddie said. 'You can't take a bit of criticism. That's pathetic. If you want to get on, you'll do what Mick says.'

'Why's he always in my face? He made me train with

the defenders. I'm a striker. I should be scoring goals.'

Eddie wasn't impressed.

'He's one of the best men on the staff. Take his advice. A team defends as a team. A striker's got to do his bit tracking back.'

I'd lost the argument, but it didn't stop me talking back. 'Mick loves himself. He's got it in for me. He keeps shoving me around.'

'All he's doing is trying to knock some sharp edges off you, Ethan. If you're going to progress you need to learn some self-discipline. You think every match is about you. You want to be the star player every time. Grow up, son. Your play is selfish. It's about the team, not the individual.'

The exchange ended there. A Mercedes Sprinter van pulled into view. I saw the tell-tale blue and yellow livery. It was the police armed response unit. They toured the estate at regular intervals.

'Get in the car,' Eddie snapped, opening the door.

I did as I was told. Eddie was angry. He didn't like being put in this position. I slid into the passenger seat and opened the window so I could hear. We watched the van pull up.

Alex hissed a warning. 'Matrix.'

Suddenly everything changed. The gang went silent. Jamie slipped away down the alley. That was the escape drill. The other boys shuffled into an untidy line, shielding his flight. A whisper went round, echoing Alex's warning.

'Matrix scum.'

Followed by a snarl of hostility.

'Bastards.'

Satisfied that Jamie had made his getaway, the older boys started to drift off.

'Stop right there, lads,' came a guttural command, barely softened by the use of the familiar greeting: *lads.*

'We haven't done anything,' Alex said, making out he was the big man.

'Nobody said you had.'

The speaker was a sergeant. His hair was shaved close at the sides, military-style. His slate-grey eyes ran over the group. Young as I was, I knew all about police stops: the clipped questions, the grunted answers.

'Empty your pockets, gentlemen.'

The boys took their time doing it. The police asked for addresses, spoke into radios, asked a few more questions. The boys moved their feet, shoved their hands in their pockets, tugged scarves a little higher over their faces only to be told to pull them down again. One of the smokers drew on his cigarette. The glowing light illuminated his gaunt features. The copper next to him tugged the cigarette from his mouth and crushed it on the pavement. It was the kind of ritual that happened most nights on the Green. It was a rite of passage for any kid on the street after dark.

'What are you up to?' the sergeant asked.

'Fashion contest.'

'Yes, we're going in for *Britain's Top Model.*'

The sergeant killed the comment with a look, but there was still the odd giggle of defiance. That's how it is on the Green. Nobody wants to lose face. When the police come, you stand your ground.

The sergeant's response was blunt. 'Let me give you a

piece of advice. Don't be here next time I come past.'

Some of his colleagues folded their arms or gave looks that said: *I'll remember your face.* There were muttered comments from the gang members. They were telling the police unit that this was their turf. The Matrix would be on their way. The gang would still be here.

Eddie watched the stand-off.

'Is this what you want, Ethan? Daily run-ins with the police, evenings spent freezing your arse off on a street corner? You want to get yourself arrested, become another stupid kid screwing up his future?'

I shook my head.

'Right answer,' Eddie said. 'This is a dead end, boy. Take my advice. Buckle down to training. Do what Mick tells you. Don't throw any more wobblers.'

He didn't understand. How could he?

I decided to eat dirt. Either that, or I was out of the Academy.

'I'll do it your way. I won't go AWOL again. Promise.'

'Good lad. I'll give you a lift home.'

'You coming, Mitch?' I called over the road to him.

'No, I'm going to stick around.'

Eddie gave me a meaningful look. Just as we pulled away from the pavement a sapphire-blue Subaru Impreza arrived. Jamie was in the passenger seat. The driver was a guy called Simmo. He was the gang leader. He didn't seem to know Jamie was after his job. There was an exchange of banter about the Matrix then three lads crowded round the car. Alex was one of them.

We were at the top of Bevan Way less than five minutes later.

'You can drop me here. Save you turning round.'

'Get an early night,' Eddie told me. 'And no more silly beggars.'

I watched Eddie's brake lights flare at the T-junction. A young mother and her son were leaving a firework display. I followed them down the street. It reminded me of when I was a kid. Images flooded my mind. I was back in a time when I didn't know the way the world worked, when I didn't understand its twisting alleys and dark shadows. Alex was running ahead with a sparkler in his gloved hand. I looked up at Mum.

'Can't we stay a bit longer?'

She shook her head.

'Just five minutes.'

'Not even one,' she said. 'It's past your bedtime.'

'Why didn't Dad come with us?'

Yes, back then I had a dad.

'He's got things to do.'

That's Declan, my dad. He always has things to do. Family isn't one of them. Rockets exploded in the sky.

'Look,' I said. 'It's raining fire.'

I wondered what Mitch was up to. We lived at opposite ends of the estate in identical rows of 1930s terraces either side of the Strand Parade. The Parade was the sickly, fading heart of the sprawling estate known to everybody who lived there simply as the Green.

We were both at Broadway High, same as Alex, same as Jamie had been, same as just about everybody else on the Green. Broadway was only five years old, built around a pentagonal design with a walkway round the open area at the centre of the school. Most of the kids said it looked like a prison. Maybe it was meant to.

There was the roar of a helicopter above us. I stopped and watched. It was training a searchlight on one of the side streets about half a mile away. The shaft of light played over the rain-slicked roofs and streets. I was still watching when the door opened. Mum saw I was alone and the light died in her eyes.

'Where's Alex?' she asked.

'He stayed out.'

'I can see that.'

'Don't get on my back,' I said, pushing past. 'I can't tell him what to do.'

Mum shoved her fingers through her mane of raven hair and shook it in frustration. Men liked her dark, almost Mediterranean features. She had soft, olive skin and fine cheekbones. That was her problem. If she'd been fat with bad skin and teeth missing the men wouldn't be interested.

They even watched her when we were with her. It made us feel invisible. From time to time I would get up and discover a strange man sitting at the breakfast table. I hated those mornings.

Mum stayed at the door staring up at the helicopter as it hovered over the estate. The searchlight continued to rove along the roads and crescents. The metallic roar of the chopper drowned the noise of the traffic.

'More trouble,' she murmured. 'I wish you'd been able to get Alex to come home with you.'

'I'm not his dad.' I was angry because of my memories. 'He's three years older than me. He doesn't take any notice.'

'Don't yell at me,' Mum said.

She bundled me inside.

'I'm not yelling.' I fought to get my anger back under control. 'You act like I'm the older brother and he's the kid. You tell me to do something about Alex. You're his mother. If he won't listen to you what makes you think he's going to listen to me?'

She sighed. 'God knows I've tried to make rules. He makes big promises then he breaks every one.' She looked defeated. 'I thought you might be able to get through to him. Sorry, love, I shouldn't be burdening you with it. I'm the adult here.'

I had things I wanted to say, but I let it go. What was the point? I lay on the couch playing Call of Duty so she didn't give me any more grief over Alex. It didn't work. She arrived with a ham sandwich and a question.

'Were you with him this evening?'

'Only for a bit.'

It was a lie. We'd been together the whole time. My thoughts kept returning to the gun. Eddie was right. Hanging round on the street was for losers.

'Who was he with?'

She would freak out if I mentioned Jamie so I picked a name that would settle her nerves.

'He was with Sean.'

That's Sean Tennant, Alex's best mate at the time.

She seemed to settle down.

'Sean's a nice lad. I've always liked him.'

Her shoulders relaxed and the tension eased from her features. She sat watching the rest of the *EastEnders* re-run. She laid her head on the arm and curled her legs under her. Just like a little girl.

She drove me crazy sometimes, but she was my mum. I loved her so much it hurt. She'd been lonely since my dad cleared off. My heart ached for her. She was a good person. She didn't deserve the betrayals, the humiliation.

I hated having to tell her lies. My half-truth that evening was just another unspoken cruelty. I hated myself for giving her false hope. I hated Alex for being one more disaster in her life. I stared out at the amber halo of the streetlamp, the beginnings of a fine drizzle. Maybe I should try to do something. I texted Alex, asked him where he was.

I waited. The drizzle turned to steady rain beating on the windows, streaming down the glass. After a few minutes my phone buzzed. I made a grab for it. Mum looked up expectantly.

Alex?

'Who was it?' she asked.

I cancelled the call and answered in a flat voice.

'Only Mitch being stupid.'

Mum's eyes dimmed. Typical Mitch. I deleted the message. He was an idiot. You didn't put stuff like that in a text. He'd just watched Jamie Leather hammer Simmo to a pulp and he couldn't wait to spill the gory details. So the Tribe belonged to Jamie now. I remembered the way he'd wrapped a powerful hand round my neck.

I went to bed about eleven, stripped to my boxers and lay on top of the duvet for a while, letting the chill work over my skin. I liked the feel of the night. Half an hour slipped by and I still hadn't heard the door. It was getting cold so I slid under the cover. As I tossed and turned, trying to sleep, I remembered the feel of the gun. Shadows crawled along the wall and slipped into the darkness that was gathering round me. I hadn't seen the last of it.

2

The morning sun was on my face. The acrid fragrance of the fireworks still hung in the air. There is always something sad about the day after Bonfire Night. It must be all those fireworks lying around like dead slugs, the sooty mist still drifting and settling. I heard something and stopped brushing my teeth. Alex stumbled into the bathroom behind me. He was wearing torn tracksuit bottoms. The zips scraped on the lino.

'What time did you get in?'

He scrubbed his stubbly scalp with his fingers and pulled at the skin under his eyes.

'Half one. Two o'clock maybe. What's with the interrogation? I only came in to take a leak.'

His pee thundered in the toilet.

'Just wondered.'

'Yeah? Well, wonder to yourself. I'm wrecked.'

'Did Mum wait up? She said she would.'

Anger lit his features.

'She flew at me the moment I walked in.'

He got angry at somebody who wasn't in the room. In Mum's absence I was the one who'd have to listen to it.

'I'm not a kid anymore. I'm seventeen. I can handle myself.'

'Jamie had a gun.'

Alex made brief eye contact.

'Keep your mouth shut about that.'

I scrubbed my lips with a hand towel. 'I'm hardly going to go spreading it around, am I?'

Alex cupped cold water and splashed it on his face. He threw some of it my way. I wanted to laugh, but I swore at him instead. That's the way we were then: always on each other's backs, some of it serious, most of it not. He was my big brother. So that was us, a family of three. Dad walked out when I was four years old and Alex was seven. Dad had smacked Mum round a bit before he left, cracked one of her ribs, gave her a black eye, a split lip and about enough self-esteem to fill a teaspoon. He was a vicious pig whose only saving grace was that he didn't use his fists when he was asleep. Declan turned up from time to time, usually when he was short of money or needed a roof over his head. He didn't stay around long. He always left hurt in his wake.

'Mitch says Jamie's number one now.'

Alex scrubbed at his tongue.

'That's right.'

I didn't want to sound curious, but I was.

'Were you there?'

He nodded. 'I saw Mitch watching. He gives me the creeps.'

'We were talking about Jamie.'

'There isn't much to tell. Jamie and Simmo had a straightener. Jamie whipped the little bitch then he shoved the Walther in his mouth.' He laughed. 'Jamie had a knuckleduster in his glove.'

'So he won by cheating.'

'You do what you have to.' He liked playing the hard man. 'You use the right tools for the job or you get whipped. You should have heard Simmo squeal. He made more noise than a stuck pig.'

He mimicked the sound of Dave Simpson gagging and whining on the gun barrel. I gave him a shut-up stare. I glanced out on the landing to make sure Mum wasn't listening.

'That how Jamie gets his kicks?'

Alex was still chuckling over the incident. 'You've got to be ruthless. He was putting Simmo in his place. No bitching about the result of the fight.'

Mum was moving around downstairs.

'Alex, Jamie's no good.'

'You didn't say that when he was showing you the gun. You were his little poodle.'

'Shut up, you.'

'What's the matter? Halo slipping? Do you think Mum's going to be disappointed in her blue-eyed boy?

He shoved me. I shoved him back.

'Knock it off.'

'Make me.'

I buttoned my shirt and knotted my tie, then pulled it down a bit. You got skitted if you looked too smart. 'I'm going to school.'

Alex yawned. 'Lucky you.'

'Here's some advice. Sarcasm's the lowest form of wit.'

'Yes, I heard.'

I shook my head and jogged downstairs. Alex had left school the first chance he got. As I opened the door to leave he was going back to bed. He wouldn't be getting up this side of midday.

Mitch and I went home via the Parade. He needed milk.

'You always have to go to the shops on the way home. Doesn't your mum do any shopping?'

Mitch shrugged. 'It would get in the way of her drinking. She doesn't do much of anything anymore. Good job breathing's involuntary or she'd be dead by now.'

Mrs Mitch was one of those grey, strained women. Maybe she'd been attractive once. Now she was thin and defeated. Her skin was the colour of wallpaper paste. She made me grateful for Mum. At least she started every day as if she wanted to live it.

We stopped at the 24/7 shop. The owner's a guy called Massoud Khan. He's OK, a bit of a pushover. Kids are always nicking from him. The 24/7 is a kind of unregistered charity. People joke that the Khans are the Green's entire ethnic minority. They're not far off. The estate is as white as Persil.

'Go pay for the milk,' Mitch said, handing me a litre carton.

I took it then tried to hand it back.

'You've got legs.'

Mitch sent a message with his eyes. I went to pay. What was he up to? I kept Mr Khan talking.

'Why's it called the 24/7 anyway? You don't open till seven and you close again at ten.'

Mr Khan gave me my change.

'I had this idea of opening round the clock, you know, the 24/7 store for the 24/7 society, but I'm in the wrong area.'

'So why not open up in the right one?'

'I can't afford the rent.'

I took the milk. The moment we were out of the door I felt Mitch tug my sleeve.

'Want a ciggie?'

'You know I hate people who smoke.'

'Cookie then.'

'You been nicking again?'

Mitch pulled the packet of biscuits out of his jacket. We sat on the wall munching the fat, sweet choc chip cookies until Mitch screwed up his face.

'I feel sick.'

'Me too.'

I threw a half-eaten cookie on the floor. 'They weren't that nice. What did you nick them for?'

'Don't know. Like the mountain, I suppose. Because they were there.'

'That your idea of kicks, stealing a packet of biscuits? You're sad, you know that?'

'You ate them.'

'I shouldn't have. I'm supposed to be eating healthy.' I pulled out my phone. 'I'm going to get my tea. I've got to be out again in an hour. Training.'

'Tonight?' Mitch was disappointed. 'I thought this was your free evening.'

'Not anymore it isn't. Mick's just increased training

from three nights to four. You should have stuck at it, you know. You're as good as me.' A grin. 'Nearly.'

'What's the point? Football's cleaned up its act. No hooliganism. The match is a family day out. They don't want kids from somewhere like the Green.'

'How do you know?' I mentioned one of our local heroes. 'He made the grade. Why not you? Why not me?'

'That was when they were still wearing bum-hugger shorts and perms. You're talking ancient history. Didn't you hear? The rich kids are taking over the world. They've got TV and the music scene boxed off. Footy will be next. Besides, they chucked me out.'

'You head-butted somebody.'

Mitch laughed. 'Yeah, I did, didn't I?'

That was Mitch all over.

'All the kid did was look at you the wrong way. Come on, hard man, I'm giving you the same look.'

'Nah, I'm not fighting you. You're my mate.'

'You daren't,' I told him. 'I'd batter you. Come on, Mitch. Do it. If you apologise, they'll let you back in. It'd be more fun with you there.'

'Ain't going to happen, Ethan. Once you start apologising, people will walk all over you.'

'What's the alternative? Do nothing? You've got to have dreams.'

That's where we were different, Mitch and me. I saw a life off the estate. He saw himself living and dying on the Green.

'Sounds like Eddie's been giving you one of his talks.'

'He gave me some good advice.'

'Why, what did he say?'

'Only that hanging round with the Tribe is the road to Hell.'

'What does he know? The Tribe will run this place one day.'

'What's to run? The estate's a pile of crap.'

'Yes, but it's our pile of crap.'

'Speak for yourself,' I told him. 'I don't owe this dump a thing. First chance I get, I'm out of here. And I won't look back.'

'Where are you going to go?'

'If I make it as a professional? I'm going to have a big, mock-Tudor house in Cheshire with a wall round it and CCTV to keep the scallies out.'

'Scallies like me, you mean?'

I laughed. 'Exactly. I wouldn't let your sort within a mile. I'll have a trophy wife with an all-the-year tan. Heated swimming pool. Ferrari out front. Lots of dogs. I'm going to have a big mob of Tosas.'

'I'll go with the wife,' Mitch said. 'If I was the next Rooney I'd get myself a supermodel. Legs that go all the way to the North Pole.'

We went quiet for a while imagining a girl with legs that went to the North Pole, then I got up off the wall.

'See you tomorrow, Mitch.'

'Yes, see you.'

Mitch took the milk home. He walked slowly. He hated school. Home wasn't much better.

Mick was at the training ground entrance. He was tall, thin, angular, the opposite of squat, grey Eddie. He had pale blue eyes like splinters from a stained glass window.

'Are you in a better mood this evening?'

'I'm OK.'

He didn't like my tone of voice.

'I like my lads to look me in the eye, Ethan.'

I picked my gaze up off the floor.

'Eddie had a word with me, said I had to play for the team.'

'I know what Eddie thinks. I need to hear from you.' He had this way of staring me out. 'You can twist him round your little finger. I want to know if you're worth the trouble. What have you got to say for yourself?'

It was swallow my pride or be thrown off the team.

'I shouldn't have got the hump. I won't do it again.' I hated Mick for making me back down. 'I'm sorry.'

He took the apology without comment.

'You're the first here. That's something in your favour. You can do your homework in the changing rooms.'

The club told us to do our schoolwork in any spare time before training.

'I haven't got any homework.'

'You sure about that?'

'I had a free period this afternoon. I'm not making it up. I've got some Spanish vocabulary to learn. That's it.'

'So study your vocab. I was good at languages myself.'

I didn't see it somehow. He wasn't that good at English!

'Spanish?'

'French. Ooh la flipping la.' He flicked a ball in the air with his toe and caught it. 'We start in fifteen minutes. Practice match. Guess what you're doing.'

'Defending,' I muttered.

'Got it in one. I'm playing you out on the right, but I want to see you tracking back. No arguing, Ethan. This isn't a democracy, it's a benevolent dictatorship and I'm getting less benevolent by the minute.'

I made my way to the changing rooms. The moment Mick was out of sight I kicked a divot out of the pitch. Eddie was getting out of his car. He saw me.

'You can knock that off,' he warned. 'There'll be no prima donnas at our club. Got enough of them in the Premiership.'

'Sorry, Ed.'

It was a night for apologies.

Mum heard the door go.

'How was training?'

'All right.'

'What's up?'

'I had to apologise to Mick.'

She waited for an explanation.

'I gave training a miss.'

I had her attention. She was used to Alex going walkabout. She didn't want me joining him.

'When?'

'Last night. Sorry.'

She muted the TV.

'Is this because he gave you a rollocking? You weren't tracking back?'

I nodded and decided to broach the other issue Mick had raised.

'He was asking after you.'

'Me?'

'A lot of the parents turn up to watch. He wondered if you'd like to come down.'

She gave a sigh of frustration. 'We've been through

26

this before. I'm a single parent, Ethan. I've always got so much to do.'

There were cups on the carpet and plates with half-eaten ready meals balancing precariously on the arms. By the door there was a pile of trainers and a pair of Mum's sandals. The wastepaper bin was overflowing. Same story with the laundry hamper in the kitchen.

'Like what?'

'Knock it off, Ethan. I'm working till five then I'm supposed to start here. You don't give me a hand and Alex is never here. I'm the only one who does anything in this house.'

I should have helped out. Life is full of should haves. I went to the fridge, looked inside and slammed the door.

'There's nothing in again.'

She looked over my shoulder and fished in her bag. 'Here. Get yourself a bag of chips.'

'I'm supposed to eat healthy.'

'Fine. Get yourself a Subway.'

'It's a half-hour walk.'

'Keep you fit.'

'I've just been training!'

She held out a ten-pound note, waved it, got huffy.

'Do you want it or not?'

I took the money and stamped to the door. She shouted after me.

'And I want the change.'

I slammed the door. When I reached the top of the street, I texted Mitch.

'Coming out? I'll stand you a Sub.'

*

Subway was on the retail park. There was a multiplex cinema, a bingo hall, a McDonald's and a KFC. We sat eating. Mitch tapped my ankle with his trainer.

'You sure your mum said you could treat me?'

'I told you, didn't I?'

'Fine,' Mitch said, ripping off a chunk of sandwich with his teeth. 'One day she's skint, the next she's buying me my tea.'

He saw a pigeon and spat the mouthful out. He laughed when the bird fluttered away before returning to peck at the bread. I watched while he repeated the game.

'That's gross.'

'Fine, I'll stop.'

He finished the sandwich. He ate hungrily, which made me wonder why he gave so much of it to the bird.

'So your mum didn't go to the shops either?'

'She's spark out on the couch. The place smells of booze.' He swallowed the final mouthful. 'You're lucky your mum doesn't drink.'

'She has a drink.'

'Yes, the odd lager. Mine runs a booze bath and climbs into it. I've never seen your mum falling down drunk like my old lady.'

He was right. Mum took care of herself. And us. Why was I so down on her?

'You're right, she doesn't get rotten.'

Mitch noticed something and twisted round.

'What is it?'

'See for yourself.'

Jamie Leather's sapphire Subaru pulled into the McDonald's Drive Thru. Alex was in the passenger seat.

They ordered Big Macs. There were five of them in the car. Jamie nudged Alex. 'There's your kid.'

Alex saw me.

'Do you want something, Ethan?'

'Just had a Subway,' I told him. 'Where'd you get the money for a Mackie's? You said you were skint.'

Alex glanced at the others in the car. 'He wants to know where we got the money.'

Everybody laughed. They were still laughing as they pulled forward to collect their order. That's when the atmosphere changed.

'NSC!'

Half a dozen shadowy figures were converging on the car park. This was the North Side Crew. They were indistinguishable from their counterparts in the Tribe. They came from the same streets. They wore the same clothes. They spoke with the same accent. But the hatred that crackled between the two gangs was as savage as it would be incomprehensible to any outsider. Things moved fast. Metal glinted in the light from a street lamp. One of the NSC boys had something in his hand. I saw it and remembered Bonfire Night.

'Alex! Watch out!'

Jamie was the first to react. He glanced over his shoulder, saw the Drive Thru was clear and reversed at high speed. He did a handbrake turn and roared away. The NSC ran into the road gesturing and shouting abuse, but the moment had gone. They wouldn't catch the speeding car.

'Was that a shooter?' I wondered out loud, barely able to believe what I'd seen.

'You're the one who shouted a warning,' Mitch said. 'Don't you know?'

It was a gun all right.

Mitch stared down the road. 'I wouldn't put anything past that maniac. He's crazy enough to go into McDonald's packing. Darren's as bad, worse. Mad bastards, the pair of them.' Then there was a note of urgency in his voice. 'Crap. They're coming over.'

We tried to make a run for it. We didn't get far. Carl brought the car round and blocked our escape.

'It's all right, Ethan,' Carl said. 'We're not going to hurt you.'

He looked for a reaction. He didn't get one.

'Tell your Alex he made the wrong choice going with Jamie Leather. He needs to watch himself. Pass the message on.'

My heart was banging. I just wanted out of there. Mitch took over and breathed defiance. 'He's not your messenger boy.'

The NSC hooted derision. 'Whoo-oo.'

Carl caught Darren's eye.

'Keep an eye on this one. He's got fire in his belly.'

Mitch was up for anything. I was tugging at his sleeve, trying to drag him away. He shrugged my hand off.

'That's right. Keep an eye on me.'

Carl stopped laughing. 'Don't push it, Mitch. I don't want to hurt you, but if you don't cut it out I will.'

'You don't scare me.' Mitch turned and walked away. I followed. After a while I glanced back.

'They've gone.' Mitch could be a liability sometimes. 'What's wrong with you mouthing off at them like that? You're crazy.'

He tossed his wrapper in the bin. 'There are worse things than being crazy. At least I'm not a coward.'

I pulled a face. 'Cowards live long lives, Mitch. Heroes wind up dead.'

That night I lay awake thinking about the gun.

3

Life slipped back into the usual routine. It was easy to think of that night outside McDonald's as something insane, a one-off, almost an unsettling dream. In many ways it was all those things. But the gun was no figment of the imagination. It was still there, waiting for somebody to call on its services. The gun will always be there. That's how it came to be offered to me. That's how I came to take it.

You find out about people on nights like that. Mitch was angry about most things and he didn't scare easily. School finally broke up for Christmas. That day winter howled across the city, scoured its way along streets, into alleys, over the waste ground. Mitch and I struggled home through horizontal, driving sleet. We leaned into the wind, blinking against its icy bite, shuddering in our thin jackets. I pulled the zip up to my nose and felt my own spit on the material.

'Doing anything over Christmas?'

Mitch grunted an answer. 'I've got a fortnight with

Mrs Happy. That's something to look forward to.'

That December afternoon he was on one of his downers. It got so he could barely speak sometimes. He rummaged in his pocket and counted the change.

'I've got enough for a Coke and a Mackie's,' he said. 'Fancy it?'

I told him no, not this time. 'I need something decent inside me before training, not a grease-out at McDonald's.'

'You're training again! They're not expecting you to practise in this weather, are they?'

'It's on as far as I know. Last session before the break.'

'Sounds too much like hard work to me. Footy's for mugs. You think you're going to get somewhere. Then, bam, they dump you.'

'That's not what happened to you, Mitch. You dumped them.'

'I wasn't talking about me.'

'Doesn't have to be that way.' I glanced at my mobile to check the time. 'I'm not going to make it as a footballer without putting in the hours.'

Mitch seemed to find that funny. 'Is that you talking? Sounds more like the Thoughts of Chairman Eddie.'

'Eddie looks out for me,' I said. 'I owe him. He's got a Cup Winners' medal. He knows what he's talking about.'

'Fine,' Mitch said. 'I'll go by myself.'

I overlooked the sulk. 'Come round ours when I get back from training. Alex got a couple of new games for the Wii.'

'Knock-off?'

'Probably.'

'Has there been any comeback, you know, after what happened with the NSC?'

'Carl Nash is top dog. Jamie's keeping his head down. Our Alex doesn't seem too impressed. He's saying he's fed up of the Tribe. He's going to give them the elbow.'

'Ain't going to happen,' Mitch said. 'He's in too deep. Jamie's like one of those alien creatures that hide in your stomach. You think you're fine then – splat. Your insides are outside.'

It wasn't the kind of picture I wanted in my head.

'Mitch, you've got a strange imagination.'

'Only telling it like it is.'

'I'll see you later, OK?'

'What time?'

'About eight?'

'Right, see you then.'

I knew there was something different the moment I walked through the door. Alex was on his way out. His jaw was set. His eyes were angry.

'Something wrong?'

'Santa's brought us an early Christmas present.'

I carried on into the living room and froze. My heart slammed. This I hadn't expected. I stared at the man lolling in the armchair. It was Declan. He looked the same as when he had walked out three years earlier. There was only one change, a new Biohazard tattoo on his right bicep. The piece of crap I was looking at was my father. Mine and Alex's.

'Hello, son.' He waited a beat. 'What, no hello for your dear old dad?'

Mum emerged from the kitchen. She had anxiety written all over her face.

'What's he doing here?' I jabbed a finger at Declan. 'Why'd you let him in?'

Mum was defensive. 'Don't kick off, Ethan. He's your dad.'

'You think?' I fixed Declan with a hostile stare. 'Real fathers stick around. What's the matter? Didn't you read that bit of the job description?'

Declan kept his eyes on me, but he didn't speak.

'Look at you,' I snarled. 'You sit there like you never went away. You don't even try to make an excuse. Don't you have a conscience?'

'Ethan,' Mum said, 'just calm down for a minute. We've just had this performance with Alex. We should talk.'

My face was burning. 'I've done my talking.'

I climbed the stairs without another word. I sat on my bed, stomach boiling with rage and confusion. My heart was thumping.

Declan. My scumbag of a dad.

He hadn't shown his face in three years. Why now? I unbuttoned my school shirt and started to get changed. I'd got training. I wasn't going to let Declan ruin things. I hurled my shirt at the wall, saw it slap against the paintwork and drop forlornly to the floor. Simultaneously, the door opened behind me. It was Mum.

'Me and Declan,' she said, 'we're going to give it another go.'

'He hit you!'

'He didn't mean it.'

'Oh, it was one of those accidental beatings, was it?'

I took a football shirt from the wardrobe and slipped it over my head. I dropped onto the bed and laced my trainers. All without saying a word.

'Ethan, you need to talk to me.'

'Will it make any difference?' I grunted, angry with

her for not even warning me. 'If I ask you to show him the door, will you do it?'

'Declan's staying.'

'Fine. He's staying. It's a done deal. So why ask for my opinion?'

She folded her arms.

'You're my son. I want to know if you're OK with this.'

'Is Alex?'

Her face seemed to crumple.

'Well, I'm not OK with it either.' A silence. 'The pig beat you. So are you going to kick him out?'

There was another silence, then: 'No.'

'Fine. You've made your decision. Look, I've got things to do. If I don't get out of the house in half an hour I'll be late for training.'

Truth is, if I didn't get out of the house I would scream. I stared down at my feet, willing her to leave. A few seconds later the door clicked shut. I felt like crap. I hoped she did too.

I lunged into the tackle. The world was madness and I was rage inside it. My studs raked the side of the attacking player's boot and sent the boy into the air, face creased with the pain of impact. I picked myself up and saw Kyle slump to the ground. He didn't spin like the footballers on TV. He just lay clutching his foot and ankle. Pain choked out of him in big, fat sobs. For a moment I didn't understand. I'd struck out at Declan. Kyle got hurt.

Mick's face appeared. It was lit with fury. 'Get off the pitch now!'

I stood my ground. The red mist still had me in its grasp. Mick marched up to me.

'Didn't you hear me? Go and get changed.' Spittle hit my face. 'I'll talk to you once I've checked on Kyle.'

I was still burning with anger. I wanted somebody to yell at.

'You said you wanted me to defend!'

'I said defend. I didn't tell you to cripple anybody. What the hell's got into you?' He pointed at the changing rooms. 'Do as I told you. Get changed. Now!'

The boiling anger was starting to drain away. It had nothing to do with Kyle. I leaned forward to ask if he was OK. Mick's eyes flashed. I raised my hands.

'OK, I get the message.'

I could feel the disapproving stares on my back. Somebody made a grab for me before being bundled away. My neck was hot. It wasn't exactly remorse, but I was feeling uncomfortable. Eddie was waiting for me.

'What was that about?'

Shame makes you stupid. You'll say anything to get off the hook. I mumbled something about mistiming the tackle.

'Don't give me that. You could have broken Kyle's ankle. You were out of order. I spend hours trying to get Mick to give you another chance and this is what you do!'

I tried to get past, but Eddie wasn't having any. He planted his feet and blocked the way.

'Oh no you don't. I know something's wrong. Talk to me, Ethan. You've always had a temper, but breaking somebody's leg isn't your style. I've never seen you go out to intentionally hurt somebody.'

I was a fish squirming on a hook.

'I was going after the ball. I got it wrong, OK? What's with everybody this evening?'

Eddie gave me one of his searching stares.

'I've already dragged you back from the brink once. Don't try my patience. Deal with me, or deal with Mick. Believe me, I'm your best option.'

Kyle was hobbling off the pitch. Mick was coming my way.

'Fine. Get Mick off my back and I'll tell you everything.'

Eddie went to intercept Mick. I heard the exchange of views, loud with wagging fingers to begin with, quieter soon after. Eddie was back in a couple of minutes.

'Follow me.'

We sat down on the steps outside the changing room.

'Thanks for dealing with Mick,' I said. 'He hates me.'

'You should be thanking him. He's just stopped Kyle's dad kicking your stupid, young head in.'

'OK. I'll apologise in a minute.'

'You'll grovel. That's what you'll do. Now spill your guts. No fairy tales. God's honest truth.'

My resistance collapsed.

'Declan's back on the scene.'

Eddie got it right away. You tell some people stuff and they forget it immediately. Not Ed. He listened.

'This is the low-life who used to knock your mum around, right?'

I nodded.

'And you think it's all going to start again?'

'I don't know. I'd got used to things the way they were. Mum holds things together. Her, me, Alex, we get along.' I buried my mouth into the neck of my shirt and mumbled through the material. 'Now Declan's back. He's not right for her, for any of us.'

'So you're angry, confused maybe. It doesn't give you the right to break a lad's leg.'

I felt a buzz of panic.

'It's not that bad, is it?'

'No, you didn't do him any real harm, but you could have.'

'I know,' I said. 'I feel sick. It's not like I planned it. I wasn't going for Kyle.'

'You wanted somebody to kick?'

I dropped my shoulders. I was starting to feel really lousy about what I'd done.

'Something like that.'

Eddie thought things over.

'Look, you get off home.'

'What about Mick?'

'I'll square it with him. It's the Christmas holidays. There's no training for two weeks. The break will give everybody time to calm down. Come back in the New Year with a different attitude.'

I nodded and went for my bus. I was going out of the gate when Eddie shouted after me.

'Any problems, you call me on my mobile, OK?'

Declan was watching cage-fighting. He heard me come in and shouted a question into the hall.

'How come you and Alex never call me Dad?'

I dropped my kit into the washing basket and turned to look at him through the open door.

'Is this a trick question? Do I get a bonus point for not laughing?'

Declan waited with uncharacteristic patience. Three years earlier he would have slapped my legs all the way upstairs and shut me in my room. The memories were bright. Fear had burned the images in my mind.

'OK,' I said, making my voice sound braver than I felt. 'Let's put this in words of a single syllable. How old was I last time I saw you?'

'Twelve?'

'Close. I was eleven. Maybe you'd like to know how I've been doing? I got fast-tracked at the Academy to play with lads a year, two years older than me. That's a real big deal. You know why they promoted me? I'm that good. Most dads would have wanted to be part of that.'

I watched for a reaction, but Declan's emotional gears were stuck in neutral.

'Glad to hear it,' Declan said finally. 'I mean it. I'm pleased for you.'

Big of him!

'You still don't get it, do you? It's not about feeling pleased. It's about being here. Do you know how I feel when I'm training? I'm the kid people are sorry for.'

'OK,' Declan drawled. 'I'm listening. Why's that?'

I snorted in disbelief. How thick was this man's skin?

'Why do you think? I don't have my parents watching me.'

Declan wasn't impressed.

'Is this where I get my violin out? Little orphan Ethan.'

'Do what you like,' I said. 'I just want you to know how I feel. There're all these dads standing on the touchline cheering their sons on. Sometimes you get one or two of the kids' mothers. There's one kid who never has anybody supporting him. That's right. It's me. Most of the lads get a lift. They drive past me as I walk home.'

I didn't care if I sounded sorry for myself. He needed to hear it.

'I bet they all talk about me in the car.'

My voice was whiny and self- pitying. I didn't care.

'Yes, that gives me a really good feeling, knowing their eyes are on me, knowing they're feeling sorry for me.'

Declan ran his right hand back over his scalp then threaded his fingers through the fingers of his left. He rolled his neck, as if easing the tension in his neck.

'I'd love to be around more, Ethan. You can't imagine how much I think about this place when I'm away.'

It was about him, the way it always was.

'Yeah, right. You're a real home-loving guy. That must have been one hell of a wrong turning. It took you three years to find your way home.'

Nothing I said, nothing I did, shook him out of neutral. Nothing. You could drill a hole in his head and you wouldn't get a reaction.

'Things aren't that easy, Ethan. I know I've been away a lot, but you have to follow the job.'

I'd had it with excuses. 'So what kind of job keeps you away this long? Three birthdays, three Christmases. How many women? Did Mum ask?'

'I'm trying to build bridges here. I didn't do this on purpose. Sometimes life doesn't work out the way you expect. OK, it wasn't just the job. Me and your mum weren't getting along too well.'

I waved away the excuses.

'That happens when you slap somebody around.'

It took him a few moments to answer.

'Don't you think I regret that every day?' he asked. He sounded almost genuine. 'Don't make me out to be the bad guy. Relationships are complicated. It takes two to get into a fight.'

I wasn't going to let that go. 'You call that a fight! A fight's a battle between equals. You're head and shoulders taller than Mum and two stone heavier.' Declan wasn't going to shift responsibility. 'I was there. You had her pinned down on the sofa and you were hitting her.' I mimicked the way he slapped her. 'Again, again, again. Alex and I were yelling at you to stop. What kind of man does that? Who beats a woman in front of her kids? You were calling her dirty names. You enjoyed it, you sick bastard.'

All the expression left his face. Even three years on I recognised the mask. Nothing has ever scared me like that blank, waxy look of his. I might be three years older, but I still flinched before him. Mum had heard us. She came and sat on the arm of Declan's chair

'Look Ethan, I know things haven't been perfect between me and your dad ...'

My senses reeled. I'd just stuck my neck out for her and here she was going to defend the scumbag.

'Listen to the woman with a PhD in understatement.'

'Let her speak, for God's sake,' Declan said.

The mask was still there.

'Or what?' I asked. 'Are you going to start on me now?' I presented myself to him, chest up, arms held out. 'Go on. Show me how you like to slap people around.'

He held my gaze. He said nothing. Part of me wanted to sting him into showing his true self. The rest of me was terrified of what I might unleash.

'I don't expect you two to become best buds,' Mum

said. 'But you can at least try to get along. Please, Ethan. Do it for me.'

I took my jacket down from the peg.

'I'm going out.'

I slammed the door behind me and pulled out my phone. I called Mitch.

'Change of plan,' I told him. 'I'm coming round yours.'

I never felt comfortable in Mitch's house. It was a pit. Plus it smelled. It stank as if something had curled up and died, but there was nowhere else to go. I didn't fancy freezing my arse off in a doorway on the Parade. I nudged Mitch and nodded in the direction of his mum.

'Does she ever *do* anything?'

'She gets wasted. Believe me, she's found something she's really good at. She should have shares in Bargain Booze.'

There was always the same catch in Mitch's voice, the result of life's daily disappointments. For a few moments we watched her staring at the TV then Mitch reached for her handbag. He eased open the clasp and pulled out a five-pound note. She carried on watching, oblivious to what he was doing.

'We're going out,' he said.

She didn't answer.

'Doesn't she get angry when you nick money off her?'

'She's off her face most of the time. She thinks she must have spent it herself.'

I wanted to know where we were going. 'I don't want to hang around the Parade again. It's bitter out.'

'I need a fix of chocolate while we think,' Mitch said. 'You? Oh no, I forgot. You're eating *healthy*.'

43

He did that inverted commas thing in the air with his fingers. We were crossing the road to the 24/7 when we saw the crowd. The revolving blue light of a paramedic's vehicle drew our attention. We wandered over.

'There's somebody on the ground,' Mitch said as he quickened his pace. There was excitement in his voice. As we got closer we could see the rain-damp tracksuit bottoms of the man on the ground, the scuffed trainers, the crumpled jacket. Then there was a face.

'That's Simmo.'

He was sitting up by the time we reached the group around him. In a few weeks he had gone from big man in the Tribe to despised loner. The paramedic was asking his name. Simmo's face was white. He looked shaken.

'What happened?' Mitch asked an elderly woman who was tutting loudly, trying to find an audience for her opinions. She turned towards him, grateful for his interest.

'Some lunatic in a car,' she said. 'He came racing down the Parade and opened his door. He knocked that lad flying.'

'What colour was the car?'

'Blue.'

Simmo was getting to his feet with the help of the paramedic. He was unsteady like a newborn foal. The police were in attendance, but Simmo was saying he was OK. His arms were flailing and he was talking fast, saying he couldn't tell them anything. He looked embarrassed and just wanted to get away.

'You can't ignore something like this,' one officer told him.

'I'm fine,' Simmo replied.

'If you know who it was, you've got to tell us.'

'I don't know anything. Honest. I didn't see who hit me.'

After a few words with the police he stumbled away, holding his side.

As the crowd thinned we moved on.

We finally found somewhere out of the wind and the cold. It was the doorway of the Beehive pub. We stood just inside the vestibule, kicking at the broken lino. Three doors opened onto it: the one that led into the street and was wedged open, then the Lounge and Bar entrances. Mitch nudged me. Somebody was coming.

'Look out, here comes Yoda.'

Yoda was an elderly man who stooped as he approached. Wiry hairs grew from the top of his ears giving him a gremlin-like appearance. The deep furrows in his brow had wrinkles of their own. Yoda shuffled past.

'Drink is the path to the dark side,' Mitch croaked. 'Drink leads to tipsiness. Tipsiness leads to falling. Falling leads to unconsciousness.'

The old guy disappeared inside. The landlord appeared a couple of minutes later and chased us out of our shelter from the storm.

'Clear off,' he ordered, 'and don't come back. I'll be checking this doorway.'

We sloped away, hands in pockets.

'You know what,' I said, 'I'm going home. I've still got homework to finish.'

I was almost home when I saw Jamie's car. The lights were on and it was parked at an odd angle. Simmo hadn't got very far. Jamie had him up against the car and was slapping him across the face. A couple of Jamie's goons were holding Simmo down. That's when I saw Alex. He was in the back of the car. He wasn't joining in, but he wasn't doing anything to stop them either. I started to hear what Jamie was saying.

'We saw you with the Beast. Did you tell them anything?'

'Nothing,' Simmo answered. 'Do you think I'm stupid?'

'Yes, I think you're stupid,' Jamie replied. 'I asked you if you said anything.'

Simmo struggled. 'And I told you no.'

Jamie slapped him again. 'Don't get smart with me.'

I didn't mean to say anything. It just came out.

'Leave him alone, eh, Jamie.'

Jamie turned. A grin crossed his face.

'Now what do you think of that, Alex? Your kid's telling me what to do.'

I tried to avoid a confrontation. 'The coppers are still around, Jamie. This is crazy.'

Jamie's eyes narrowed. 'Did you just call me crazy?'

I froze. I could have chosen my words better. Jamie let go of Simmo and walked over.

'Did you call me crazy?'

His eyes were blazing.

'I didn't mean it like that.'

'Funny, that's how it sounded to me.'

Alex got out of the car.

'Maybe he's right, Jamie. Why don't we leave it, eh?'

Jamie fixed me with a cold stare then glanced over his shoulder at Alex.

'You'd better not be going soft on me, Alex.'

'It's not that. The police have scraped Simmo off

the pavement once tonight. There's no point drawing attention to ourselves.'

Jamie glanced at the other guys in his crew and got shrugs that seemed to support what Alex had said. He patted my cheek.

'Fine.'

He shoved Simmo off the car and got in. The others followed.

He gave his victim a parting shot. 'You know what happens to grasses.'

I caught Alex's eye before they drove off. Simmo was unsteady on his feet.

'You OK?' I asked.

He was holding his ribs. 'I've been better.'

His face was red where Jamie had slapped him.

'Do you need a hand getting home?' I asked.

He shook his head.

'Sure?'

'Yes, I'm sure.'

I was turning the corner when I heard his voice.

'Hey, Ethan,' he said. 'Thanks.'

4

Next day there were blizzards. Ghostly white flakes danced against an end-of-the-world sky. When the storm abated, a bright, hard sun emerged and the estate came to life. Kids had snowball fights in the street. Cars slithered to a halt and kerbed wheels. Exhausts spewed white vapour. People skidded down the path with their shopping, clung to gate posts, fell. By evening lights were winking through the indigo darkness. The sky bore down on the whiteness of the falling snow. The Green seemed to metamorphose. This most unmagical of places discovered a kind of bleak enchantment.

It seemed to infect the house. For once we were all home at the same time. Alex was watching TV in that lazy, detached way of his. Mum and Declan were sprawled on the sofa. She had her legs stretched over him and he was stroking her bare toes. I messed with my phone, scrolling through the messages for no other reason than to block out their show of intimacy. Didn't she have any pride? No matter how often he let her down she came back for more.

'Tell you what,' she announced. 'Why don't I cook a proper Christmas dinner this year, turkey and all the trimmings?'

Declan got all excited. Wonderful, I thought, you beat your woman, but you go all teary-eyed over Crimbo. It was the sentimentality of the psycho.

'I can get us a cheap turkey,' he said. 'A lad at work knows somebody.'

'Local turkey thief?'

Mum went to say something, but Declan stopped her with a slight shake of the head. She forced some brightness into her voice.

'There you go,' she said. 'Declan gets the turkey. I cook it. Call me Nigella.'

Alex faked choking with astonishment.

'You ... cook?'

'I can cook.'

'Yes, you *can*, but you don't. You heat stuff up in the microwave.'

'You're always starving when I get in from work.' She stared down any other smart comments. 'We're going to sit down round the table like a real family.'

The Holts weren't known for playing happy families.

'You sure about this? In the soaps they always have fights and murders at Christmas.'

'This isn't a soap,' Mum told me pointedly.

I met the comment with my idea of a meaningful silence. Alex was quiet too, suppressing thoughts that could too easily spring to his lips. After a few minutes he got up and wandered into the kitchen. I followed him.

'Listen to her,' he growled. 'He hasn't changed. This is going to end in tears.'

'He's a pig. He's going to let her down same as always.'

Alex slammed an open cupboard door to express his frustration.

'Who said he could just walk back in and take over the place? He acts like he's lord of the manor.'

I let him rant. A scabby little house in Bevan Way wasn't much of a manor to lord over. Mum shouted for us to put the kettle on.

Alex spooned instant into two mugs, poured on boiling water and added a splash of milk. I thought he was going to spit in it, but he managed to be polite to Declan. He even got a thank you. It was all too good to be true.

Mum cooked her Christmas dinner. There was a table set up in the living room. It had a red paper tablecloth edged with holly and ivy. There were candles in little holders and crackers and party hats and Mariah Carey and Coldplay singing Christmas songs. The only thing missing was a fat guy in wellingtons.

Alex gave his verdict. 'Just like a real Christmas dinner.'

'The sort real families have.'

The turkey was dry and the roast potatoes came out of a bag in the freezer, but all in all it wasn't a bad effort. Declan made the gravy. It had a spoonful of curry paste and lots of black pepper.

'Well?' Declan asked.

'Yes,' Alex said grudgingly, 'it's not half bad.'

Mum left the room to fetch pudding and Declan went with her.

Alex said, 'Did we call this wrong, Ethan? You don't think he could stick around this time? He should be well gone by now.'

How was I supposed to answer? It was simple when

I knew Declan was just going to parachute in then leave Mum shattered and lonely like he always had before. It's easy when it's familiar. You know how to react. You're surly, resentful, prickly. You rebuff every attempt Declan makes to build bridges. But days were turning into weeks and Declan was still there. There was something new in the air. Declan was keeping control of his temper. Mum was happier than any time I could remember.

'I don't get it either.'

So what do you do when the bad guy doesn't turn out so bad after all? When the monster starts acting like a pussycat? When do you start returning the smiles in spite of yourself? When do you start to trust the scumbag? Just asking the questions made me even more certain I was being stupid. Men like Declan didn't change. It was only a matter of time before he showed his true colours.

'He'll be gone in the New Year,' I told Alex. 'You watch.'

It was safer to hate Declan and prepare for the worst. That way you don't get hurt.

'Leopard hasn't changed his spots then?'

'Is that a trick question? Where's he been for the last three years? Why doesn't he say something?'

Alex turned over what I'd said. 'You're right. He hasn't changed. Same old scum.'

I heard footsteps.

'Watch out,' I whispered, 'here come the happy couple.'

We finished the meal and sat looking at each other. Declan broke the silence.

'There's a cracker left,' he said. 'Who wants to pull it with me?'

Alex snorted. 'Forget it. I'm seventeen.'

Declan looked at me.

'And I'm fourteen. We're not kids anymore.'

'Go on, it's Christmas. What about it, son?'

For once I didn't react when Declan called me son. I saw the hope in Mum's face. She had put her heart into making this dinner special. Maybe that's why I weakened. OK Mum, I thought.

For you.

Not him.

Declan held out the cracker and raised his eyebrows. It snapped, leaving me with the longer end.

'You win,' Declan said.

I said nothing. That remained to be seen.

Alex let himself into my room.

'Don't you ever knock?'

'Why, what are you up to in here?'

'Nothing, but this is *my* room. I've got a right to some privacy.'

'Oh, we want rights now.'

Something was eating him. Why was he being like this?

'I just think you should knock, that's all.'

Alex kicked the door shut behind him.

'And I think you should stop sucking up to Declan. I thought you wanted shot of him, same as me.'

'I do.'

'Yeah, looks like it.' He could do sarcasm like nobody else. 'Pull a cracker with me, *son*.'

My flesh prickled.

'What was I supposed to do?'

'Tell him to stick his stupid cracker. That's what I did.'

I turned to escape his gaze and muttered a retort. 'Yes, you're a real hero.'

'You're pathetic, Ethan, you know that. You were the same when you were a kid.'

His words acted as a key opening a door in my mind. Suddenly, it was as if a shaft of light had lanced across a darkened room.

'What's that supposed to mean?'

'Forget it.'

'No, I want you to explain yourself.'

Alex took his time answering.

'Remember that time he hurt her, I mean really hurt her?'

In the shaft of light there were two figures. They were struggling. It was an image that had flitted in and out of my nightmares for years, a blurry uncertain image of a terrible time.

'Of course I remember. Who do you think you're talking to?'

He snorted. 'You know. You *know*. You were weak then and you're weak now.'

He made for the door. I beat him to it and slammed it as he yanked it open.

My palm was against the wood, holding it shut. My stare was on Alex.

'You're going to tell me what you mean by that!'

'Got a short memory, haven't you, little brother? Maybe you just remember what you want to remember.'

Half-formed pictures stuttered through my imagination, reminders of a version of me I didn't want anyone else to see. Alex was hurting because of his memories. He wanted me to hurt too and he had the weapons to do it. He saw the horror in my face as the past came bubbling up like filthy water.

'You've got it now, haven't you?'

'Get out!'

He laughed. 'Oh, you want me out now, do you?' He turned. 'Well, I'm not going. You'll hear me out. Declan was slapping her. Remember that? He's got a hand like a spade and it kept coming down again and again. You expect a blow like that to be loud, but it isn't, is it? Her body took the whole impact. There was this thick, heavy slap like somebody pounding meat. I've never heard anything like it.'

Every detail was chillingly perfect. That's exactly what it was like. My knees gave way under me and I sat on the edge of the bed.

'She was grunting with pain at every slap and every punch. She was sobbing. There was this one blow made her throw her head back. She saw us standing in the doorway. She swallowed her screams. She did it for us, so we wouldn't be scared.' He opened the door. 'You were the youngest. She wanted to protect you most.' His voice was bitter. 'She did it for you, Ethan, because you're *the sensitive one*.'

I didn't want to hear it, but I had to know the rest.

He stood over me.

'I was screaming at Declan to stop. I was trying to pull him off her, but he was too strong. I yelled for you to help me.'

His words made me flinch. I could see the younger me standing in the doorway while Alex clawed at Declan, trying to drag him away. I knew what Alex was going to say next.

'Together, maybe we could have done something. I don't know.' He said it in despair as he remembered his helplessness. Then the anger returned. 'But you just stood there, didn't you? I wanted you to bring me my baseball bat to give me a fighting chance. You just stood there sobbing your eyes out. You were feeble, Ethan.'

'I was only eleven.'

'And I was fourteen. So what? I was a kid too. Don't you think I was scared? You're trying to make excuses. I pleaded with you. I yelled at you to bring the bat, but you just stood there. Declan didn't forget what I said about the cricket bat. He enjoyed using it to punish me later. But he didn't punish you. You were on his side.'

'That's not fair, Alex. I would have done anything to stop him hurting Mum.'

'Easy to say, harder to do.'

Even then he wasn't done. He hit me with one last blow. 'Maybe I could have forgiven you for being a coward. Being scared isn't a crime. It's what you said after it was over.'

This time I didn't remember. I raised my face.

'I don't understand.'

'Seriously?'

'I mean it. I don't remember.'

'You mean you don't want to. If I was in your shoes, I'd bury it deep.'

Alex folded his arms. He told his story quietly, letting every word sink in.

'Declan went out for a drink. He came back unsteady on his feet, but he was strong enough to use that baseball bat to remind me who was boss.'

In my mind's eye Alex was cowering on the kitchen

floor while Declan laid about him with the bat.

'You didn't do anything to help me either. He must have hit me half a dozen times before Mum put herself in the way.'

'But what was it I said?'

'You really don't know?'

'No.'

'It's like this,' Alex told me. 'I helped Mum clean herself up. You could have asked how she was, anything. Instead, you asked her if she was splitting up with Dad. She was cut and bruised and you were begging her not to send him away. You thought we could all go back to playing Happy Families. I couldn't believe my ears. I wanted to kill you.'

'I only meant I wanted them to be together, happy the way they used to be. That's how all kids feel.'

'I didn't! I could see what it was doing to Mum.'

'I wouldn't let anybody hurt her.'

'No? Well, it didn't look like that from where I was standing. I needed you to be strong Ethan, and you were weak. I needed an ally and you were a pathetic, whining kid.'

'I was eleven!'

'So you keep saying. You didn't let us down because you were young. You let people down because you're weak. I'll never be weak the way you are. Never!'

This time he was going. But he had one last thing to say.

'Of course, the joke's on you. There was no happy ending. Declan stayed around long enough to hurt her again then he cleared off anyway. I don't just want him to go, Ethan. I want him to die. If there was a way I could get away with it, I would do it with my own hands.'

After he left I felt more alone than I had ever felt in my life.

Mitch was with me when I arrived home from school the following afternoon. I was glad of the company. I wasn't ready to face Alex on my own. What if he raked everything up in front of Mum? Mitch was my protection. He didn't say so, but he wanted somewhere to hang out. His mum was having one of her bad weeks. I could always tell. She would sit staring at a point in the mid-distance, kind of quivery and distracted. We turned into Bevan Way.

'So she's drinking again?'

'She's started bringing home these big bottles of cheapo cider. They're everywhere.'

I opened the door.

'Have you eaten, Mitch?'

His face was a picture of humiliation. 'Toast. There's never anything in.'

Mum was waiting in the hallway. 'I thought it might be Alex,' she said.

I had a bad feeling in my gut.

'What do you mean? Hasn't he been in?'

'He hasn't been home all night.'

'What, no phone calls? He's gone missing?'

I saw the tell-tale look and ushered Mitch into the kitchen.

'Is it OK if Mitch has something to eat?'

It seemed to take a few minutes for Mum to register the question. She nodded absently.

'Of course. There are sausages and eggs in the fridge and some crusty bread. Do a fry-up for yourself, Mitch. Ethan and I need to talk.'

Mitch frowned, wondering what was going on. Curious doesn't do justice to the expression on his face. He made himself scarce in the kitchen.

'So what's the deal with Alex?' I asked.

'He hasn't been home,' she whispered again. 'I'm worried sick.'

Did it have something to do with our quarrel?

'Declan took the day off work to look for him. He's out searching.'

That was going to help!

'Alex didn't text or anything?'

'Nothing. I've been up half the night. I tell you, I'm worried sick.'

'Don't worry about Alex.' I squeezed her arm. 'He's fireproof. Look, he'll be OK. He probably dossed somewhere.'

'Like Jamie Leather's house?'

It was a name I'd been trying to avoid.

'I wish he wouldn't have anything to do with that family. Jamie gives me the creeps. It's those eyes. There's no life in them. God knows the whole brood is rotten to the core.' She ran a hand through her black hair. 'If Alex was in hospital somebody would have rung, wouldn't they?'

I shrugged.

'What if he's in trouble with the police?'

'They would have called you, surely.'

'I don't know.' A sigh. 'Maybe. If he doesn't turn up soon I'm calling them.'

Mitch appeared at the door.

'Toast or bread with your fry-up?'

'Toast.'

'Do you want anything, Terri?' he asked, trying to elbow his way into our conversation.

Mum shook her head.

'I've been racking my brains, wondering where he is. I can't think of anything.'

That's when the door went. Declan walked in. Alex was with him.

'You get your tea with Mitch,' Mum said. 'I want to hear what he's got to say for himself.'

It was my turn to walk unannounced into Alex's room.

'Is this because we fell out?'

The frown told me I was wide of the mark.

'Don't be stupid. Not everything is about you, Ethan.' He was agitated. He couldn't keep his hands still. 'Come in. Shut the door behind you.'

He wasn't angry with me anymore.

'What's wrong?'

'It's Jamie. He got arrested.'

'It's not the first time.'

'This is different.'

I wondered: different how?

'And you were with him?'

Alex gave a guilty nod.

'Did you get arrested?'

Alex blew hard, puffing out his cheeks. 'No. I got away. It's all because of Simmo.'

I listened. That was a name I hadn't heard in a while.

'I thought Simmo was supposed to be a spent force.'

'He's a turncoat. He's gone with the North Side Crew. It's his way of getting back at Jamie.'

'So Jamie decided to teach him a lesson?'

'Pretty much. We caught up with him on the Parade. A car dropped him off. It belonged to Carl Nash. We waited until Nash had gone then we jumped him.'

'How bad did you hurt him?'

Alex shook his head. 'Bad.'

'You could do time for this!'

'I thought it was just a warning,' Alex said. 'Only Jamie went mental. He got Simmo on the floor and started kicking him in the ribs. Ethan, he stamped on his face. You could see Simmo's eyes roll back in his head. I felt sick.'

'Didn't you try to stop him?'

Alex shook his head slowly. 'I just stood there … I kind of froze.'

'Like me when Declan hurt Mum.'

Alex stared in disbelief. 'I can't believe you brought that up. Are you trying to use what happened tonight as an excuse for what you did?'

I dropped my eyes. That was stupid. 'No. Sorry.' Then I stopped talking about myself. 'You're an accessory. Jamie's a major liability. Have you forgotten Bonfire Night? That wasn't a replica. Jamie's into guns in a big way. He gets a kick out of hurting people.'

Alex had his head down.

I broke the silence. 'Finish your story.'

'The police car had its lights flashing. Somebody must have seen us and tipped them off. We scattered. Jamie went one way. Sean and I went the other. Jamie got unlucky and ran straight into the path of a second police car.'

'He was the only one arrested?'

'Yes, it was just Jamie. He's the one they were after.

You don't know how long they've been trying to take him down.'

I whispered a piece of advice.

'You need to tell Mum something that's going to settle her nerves. She's been climbing the walls.'

'Not easy.'

'Why didn't you come home?'

Alex took his time answering.

'I don't know. I wasn't thinking straight. I had to get off the street before the police picked me up too. I followed Sean. We were close to his house so I asked if I could crash there. I felt too ashamed to go home.'

'You could have phoned.'

'I know. I should have. I wasn't thinking straight.'

'You've got to get out of the Tribe, Alex. If you carry on hanging round with Jamie you're going to go down.'

5

It wasn't like Eddie to turn up unannounced. I opened the door to him and felt the sting of the winter wind on my face. Watery sunlight gleamed on the windows of the houses opposite. Stray snowflakes nestled in Eddie's coarse, grey hair. I waited for him to speak. It had to be bad news.

'Is it the tackle? Am I getting kicked out of the Academy?'

Breathless. Panicky. The end of football was the end of me.

Eddie stamped the snow from his shoes. The January cold had pinched his nose traffic-light red.

'You couldn't be further from the truth,' he said. 'Have you got a passport? You're going to the States.'

My heart thumped. The States? Mum arrived behind me.

'Did you say the States?' she asked. 'As in America?'

Eddie's eyes twinkled. 'Give the lady a prize. She just knocked the coconut off its stand.' Eddie, usually as gruff as he was squat, was in a hearty mood.

I didn't know what to think. 'The USA. Are you kidding? This is a wind-up. It's got to be.'

Eddie nodded in the direction of the living room.

'Can we sit down and talk it over? If I stand here much longer I'm going to turn into an ice cube.'

'Of course,' Mum said. 'You must think we're really rude.'

She led the way indoors. Declan was channel-surfing listlessly. I saw the way Eddie scrutinised his features. I wasn't the only one who didn't believe cuckoo boy's conversion from Dark Lord to Jedi.

'This is my partner, Declan,' Mum said.

Eddie nodded curtly. Declan held out his hand and Eddie took it. The handshake had all the enthusiasm of a polar bear that's just won a month's holiday on the Costa Brava.

'The club is going to send a team out to play in a youth tournament in Dallas.'

Eddie breezed on. He was enjoying being the bearer of good news.

'The lads stay with families connected with the Dallas youth set up. Ethan will be out there for two weeks. That's if you agree of course, Mrs Holt.'

Mixed emotions shifted across Mum's face.

'What's it going to cost?'

'Don't worry about that,' Eddie answered. 'The club picks up the tab. It's a wonderful opportunity for the boy.'

My heart was pounding harder than ever. America.

'When is it?'

'During the Easter holiday. He won't miss any school.'

Declan laughed. 'You wouldn't care about that, would you Ethan?'

I rounded on him. 'Who asked your opinion?'

Eddie listened with interest. His gaze flicked across to Declan who shrugged, reached for his jacket and headed for the door.

'I'm going for a pint.' Declan paused on the way out. 'You really think Ethan's that good? There could be money in it?'

He realised he had struck a bum note.

'I mean Ethan could make a good living. I'm thinking of the boy's future.'

'Yes, if everything goes right he could make a living out of football. You have to understand – Ethan's a young lad. He does it for the love of the game. Nothing else.'

Declan hesitated for a moment, aware he had been slapped down, then stepped out into the howling cold.

'You'll get a pack in the post,' Eddie said, still distracted, frowning after the striding Declan. 'There will be permission forms, details of the families offering accommodation, information about the tournament. I just wanted to come round and give Ethan the good news, Mrs Holt.'

'Call me Terri.'

'Terri it is,' Eddie said. 'Ethan will have to write a letter about himself, his hobbies and interests, that kind of thing. It will help the Dallas people place him with the most suitable family.'

'You're OK with this, aren't you Mum?'

The answer wasn't long coming.

'Of course I am.' She turned her gaze in Eddie's direction. 'Does this mean he could really make it?'

'The raw talent's there,' Eddie said. He seemed to like the way she talked about ambition rather than money, the way Declan had. That was Mum. Even when she drove me crazy, she never wanted anything for herself, only Alex and me. Declan was her only vice. 'You've got a good lad here, Mrs Holt. If he works hard and listens to the coaching staff there's no saying how far he could go. I haven't seen many young lads hit the ball as sweetly as this son of yours. He's a natural.'

My heart swelled with pride. I didn't get to feel good about myself very often so this was a big day. Eddie didn't spread the praise too thickly. I had one more question.

'And Mick's OK with this?'

'He's the one who nominated you,' Eddie answered.

This really was news.

'Mick did!'

'You shouldn't be surprised. You've got him all wrong, Ethan. Forget the tough exterior. Mick's a stand-up guy when you get to know him. He comes down on you like a ton of bricks because he thinks you're worth the trouble. The way he sees it, you need a bit more self-control and a lot less lip.'

Eddie clamped a strong hand round the back of my neck. It brought back the night Jamie had done the same. I was used to feeling a guiding hand. Pity none of them belonged to my own dad.

'He knows you're a prospect, Ethan. We all do.' He glanced at Mum. 'I'm going to put my cards on the table, Terri. This son of yours has got more ability than anyone I've scouted, but he's got more attitude than most. He's got to learn to direct that energy in the right direction.'

Eddie's hard gaze was on me.

'Your fight isn't with Mick, son. It's with yourself.'

We talked for another quarter of an hour. Mum put

questions to Eddie. Eddie gave detailed answers to every one. When he had gone I Googled Dallas. I read every word of the Wiki entry. I could hardly believe I was going to be in Texas in a few months' time.

Mitch wanted to celebrate. He disappeared into the kitchen. The house was worse than ever. His mum seemed to have given up completely. There was a strange smell, a kind of moist, sickly sweet odour. It turned my stomach. Mitch returned proudly grasping the neck of a cheapo bottle of cider. I examined the label.

'This stuff's lethal,' I said.

'Yes, but it gets you off your head. Do you want some?'

I held out my mug.

'Why not? I'm going to *America*. Where's your mum anyway?'

'She's got some feller across town. Another stupid alchy. They get hammered together. I haven't seen her for two days.'

He was slagging his mum off as an alchy then downing pints of rotgut cider himself. The cider clucked in the mug as Mitch poured. I held up a hand, but Mitch just carried on pouring. I took a sip and grimaced.

'This is like raw sugar.'

Mitch read the label.

'Raw alcohol more like.'

It wasn't long before we were roaring drunk. I rummaged through the CDs in the wall unit. Susan Boyle, Take That and an *X Factor* compilation went in the rejects pile. I snapped the most recent disc I could find into the player. Then we were punching the air and singing.

We reeled into the street, still singing, and set off with

no particular place to go. We passed a fence. A mongrel with a recognisable streak of Alsatian hurled itself at the gate, snarling and snapping. We kicked at the gate. The racket brought the owner to the door. He started yelling.

'You should keep your dog under control,' Mitch said.

He gave the fence another almighty kick and his trainer crashed through the rotten plank.

'Right you,' the householder shouted, coming after us.

I was already on my toes. Mitch's trainers were thudding behind me. He rolled a wheelie bin in front of our pursuer. I heard a loud *ouf* of discomfort. He was carrying a lot of weight. Michelin Man soon fell back. I skidded round a corner. Mitch caught up. I panted a question.

'Is he still there?'

Somewhere in my alcohol haze Eddie's worn features were frowning disapproval.

'Nah, we lost him,' Mitch replied. 'He's probably having a heart attack somewhere. See the state of him. If I let myself get in that state, you can kill me there and then. What a lard-arse.' He pulled up his trouser leg. He was bleeding. 'I cut myself on that fence.'

We were so drunk we found it funny.

'Teach you to go booting it.'

That set us off again. Then I felt acid coming up my throat. I vomited violently.

'There you go,' Mitch said. 'That's how you celebrate going to America.'

Alex covered for me when I got home.

'I told Mum you'd got the runs. Something you ate.' He laughed. 'Not something you drank.'

67

I was sitting on the side of the bath, feeling sorry for myself.

'You going to be sick again?'

'Don't know. Maybe.'

I had a pounding headache after my boozy evening with Mitch. I didn't know it was possible to feel this bad. My head was throbbing. I was dehydrated and weak and my stomach winced at the very thought of food. If this was a hangover you could keep it.

'I thought you had to stay fit.'

The rough, bitter taste on my tongue and the dull, empty throb in my head said I would never feel fit again.

'I thought you were trying to be helpful.'

Alex was laughing. 'I am, but it's fun watching you suffer!'

I glared at him. 'I'm an idiot. I let Mitch talk me into drinking cider.'

'The white stuff?'

A nod.

'Phew, bad choice.'

'I'll never listen to him again.'

'You can't blame it all on Mitch. It doesn't look like you took much persuading.'

I cupped water into my mouth and spat. I rinsed my nostrils and snorted it out.

'Where'd you get the booze?' Alex asked.

'His old lady's got a stash. The place is like a brewery.'

'She won't be too pleased when she sees you've cleared her out.'

'Most of the time she's too off her face to know what's going on. You could sell her furniture from under her and she wouldn't notice.'

Alex tugged at his earlobe.

'No wonder Mitch has turned out such a loser.'

I changed the subject.

'Any news about Jamie?'

'He's pleading guilty. He hasn't got much choice. With his track record he'll be lucky to get a suspended sentence.'

'So he's going down?'

Alex nodded.

'Nothing so certain.'

'What happens to the Tribe when he's gone?'

There was one of those long silences when you hear the rumble of traffic in the distance.

'None of my business,' Alex said. 'Not anymore.'

For a moment I almost forgot to feel sick.

'You mean you've quit?'

'Let's say I'm feeling a bit semi-detached. I thought I knew what made Jamie tick. That night I saw another side to him. He could have killed Simmo.'

'The NSC boys will rule the estate.'

Alex turned to go.

'Like I said, it's got nothing to do with me anymore.'

I would never forget those strange, unsettling months of promise and hope before the return of the gun. They would haunt me through the days of rage and fire to come. I remember it as a time of peace, almost a happy time. Almost every day I expected Declan to up sticks and leave Mum crushed and bereft. It didn't happen.

Almost every day I expected Alex to return to the Tribe. That didn't happen either. Alex shook himself free. He didn't want to admit it, but the change at home seemed to make it easier to cut loose. Mum was happier than either of us had seen her for years. The Tribe was unravelling. With a prison term looming, there was nothing Jamie could do to prevent it breaking up. All the while, the prospect of the tournament in Dallas came ever closer, taking on solid shape, transforming itself from dream to reality, elbowing its way into my thoughts.

February relaxed its icy grip. Declan was still there. Mum was happy. Alex was even looking for work. I helped him do a CV. One March day I opened the door and walked in on complete uproar.

'What gives?'

'I've only gone and got myself a job,' Alex said.

I must have looked sceptical.

'This isn't a wind up. Sean's dad knows a plumber. He's part of a general construction firm. Anyway, he got Sean an apprenticeship. Sean asked if there were any more jobs going. They asked me to go for an interview. Six lads applied and I was the one who got it.'

I looked around as if for confirmation. Mum and Declan were nodding.

'Well, what do you reckon?' Alex asked. 'I've never come first in anything in my whole life.'

I launched myself at him and started to rub the top of his head with my knuckles. Alex howled with laughter. Declan joined in. Alex was laughing so much, he didn't seem to notice. Declan had an idea.

'Let's go for a meal? Where will it be, Alex?

'Nando's.'

Declan patted Alex on the shoulder. 'Good choice, son.'

Alex reacted as if he had been burned with a branding

iron. Declan got the message and removed his hand.

An hour later we were sitting in front of a platter of Piri Piri chicken. The chicken sizzled. We exchanged banter. Mum sparkled. Then Alex got a text. His face changed.

'What now?' Mum asked. 'It's trouble, isn't it?'

Her voice was thick with anxiety.

'It's nobody.'

'I'm not buying it, Alex. I want to know who sent you a message.'

He nodded his surrender.

'It was Dean.'

Dean Leather. Jamie's younger brother.

'And?'

'It's Jamie. He's just got two years.'

'For assaulting Simmo?'

'Yes.' The news unlocked something in Alex. He started to talk and tell us stuff he had never mentioned. 'It wasn't just assault. I've never told anybody the full story.' I could hear the shame in his voice. 'He had a set of knuckledusters and some wraps on him.'

'Drugs? What kind?'

'Does it matter?'

Mum's face said it did, but she would leave the interrogation for later. Alex continued his story.

'He could have got a shorter term, but he wouldn't grass on his mates.'

Mum gave her judgement. 'Well, I think the court did its job.' Her voice was indignant. She hated the way there was still a trace of respect in the way Alex talked about Jamie. 'That boy is no good, Alex. Jamie Leather is where he belongs. You're better off without him.'

Alex shoved his chicken round the plate.

'You're right, but—'

'There is no but!'

'I still feel bad. He's my mate.'

Mum reacted fiercely. 'He isn't your friend. He's a complete psycho. You should never have got involved with him.'

'It's not like it makes any difference what any of us thinks,' Alex said. 'I won't be seeing him for a while.'

Mum wasn't satisfied. She didn't just want the door closed on Jamie Leather. She wanted it barred and bolted. 'You shouldn't be seeing him *ever*.'

It went quiet. Declan's gaze wandered round the group.

'What say we find out what they do by the way of desserts in this place?'

There were nods all round.

Dessert was sweeter than Jamie Leather.

That same day, not a mile away, half a dozen soldiers from the Tribe huddled under a street lamp. The industrial estate was derelict and there was only one light working in a line of six. Dean Leather marched smartly down the row of disused units. The buildings had been empty for the best part of two decades. Paint flaked. Rust stippled ironwork. Here and there it was possible to make out the staccato tap of dripping water. The buildings were the skeletal remains of better times when machines hummed, phone operators took orders, white vans roared out of loading bays. Dean stopped where the road was darkest. He pulled a key from his tracksuit bottoms and knelt down. Glancing left and right, he inserted it in a padlock at the bottom of the roller doors. When it wouldn't turn he cursed.

'It's rusted up like Jamie said. Bring me that can of WD40.'

He sprayed the lock then inserted the key again. He twisted it this way and that, applied some more WD40 then smiled as it opened. He shoved up the roller doors about a metre until they stopped with a protesting squeal. When they wouldn't go any further, he ducked his head and rolled inside.

He used the backlight from his mobile phone to find the steel shelving where Jamie had told him to hide the Walther pistol. Dean unzipped his jacket and pulled out the gun. It was wrapped in cloth and bound with two big, fat elastic bands. There was a blue steel toolbox just as Jamie had said. He flipped the catches, lifted the tray, shoved the gun underneath and replaced the box. He snapped the catches back down and rolled back outside. As he pulled the door down and secured it, he glanced at the others.

'Anybody mentions this place, they'll have to explain themselves to Jamie when he gets out. You don't mouth off. You don't boast, not even to your girlfriend. Got that?'

There were nods all round. Jamie was on his way to prison. He wasn't dead. He wouldn't serve much more than half the sentence if he behaved himself. Nobody was going to risk making an enemy of somebody who would be back on the Green in fourteen, eighteen months at most.

The gun would remain in the lock-up, waiting for Jamie.

It still had work to do.

6

I sat on the edge of the bed. Not my bed. An American bed. I couldn't believe I was there. Dallas. Texas. Easter in the USA. When I walked across the Green I knew every brick of the place. The places were full of memories: the good, the bad, all too often the ugly. I felt the whip of the wind, the thud of my footsteps on a pavement stiff with familiarity. I was part of the harsh, shifting world of the Green.

The hours of long-haul Atlantic flight had been different. Sealed in a steel tube, I had felt removed from everything I knew. I didn't really have any sense of going anywhere, just the strange hum of this anaesthetised tube in the sky. I was insulated from the world that was rushing thousands of metres below. Some of the others bobbed up and down excitedly. I stayed in my seat, watching the sky map of the journey, the almost meaningless distances involved. It felt unreal.

The room was all clean lines. There was no clutter, none of the never-quite contained chaos of home. There was a TV and a Mac. Family photos competed for space with two giant pinecones, an iPod, a baseball mitt and a science calculator. I tried to work out what all the keys were for. There were pennants on the wall. FC Dallas. Dallas Cowboys. America's team. Soon there was a knock. My host, Mr Morrison, poked his head round the door.

'Are you settling in OK?'

'I haven't unpacked yet. I still can't believe I'm here.'

Mr Morrison seemed to find that funny.

'You're here all right. Welcome to the good old US of A. Pinch yourself if you like.'

I surveyed my surroundings.

'Whose room is this?'

'It's my son John's.'

He explained that John was at university.

'I'd like to go to university.'

'Go for it.'

'I will,' I said.

Just like that. As if I had the slightest clue how to turn hope into reality. People from Broadway did go to uni. There was a board in the school foyer recording the successes. Until this moment I had never quite been able to imagine myself as one of them, no matter how I tried.

'What will you study?'

'I don't know.'

'Keeping your options open, right?'

That was the difference between me and the boy whose room I was occupying. He would have had a plan. All I had was a half-baked idea, hazy, unfocused, the ghost of a dream. Somehow I couldn't imagine going to university, but I couldn't imagine not going either. There was something about this room that said university wasn't a dream, it was an entitlement. Going on to study was as natural as waking up with the Texan sun filtering through those curtains. It must be easy to succeed growing up in this spacious, beautiful house. It was a long way from the Green.

'You make yourself right at home, Ethan.'

'I will. Thank you.'

'The burgers are on the barbecue,' Mr Morrison told me. 'Come out in the yard when you're ready.'

I was ready then. The airline food had left me starving. I brushed my teeth, tugged at my shirt and gave it a sniff. I sprayed deodorant, killed time for a few moments so I didn't look too eager, then wandered out into the yard. The 'yard' was more like a field bordered by trees I didn't recognise, not that I recognised many trees. I decided they were cowboy trees. Growing up on the Green didn't make you Nature Boy. Mr Morrison had fixed lights in some of them and they bathed the scene with a melting yellowish glow that added to the sense of unreality.

Mr Morrison introduced his wife and daughters. I forgot the name of the younger one instantly. She was all ponytail and freckles and saccharine sweetness. I wasn't about to forget the older girl's name. Carrie. She was like something out of a dream too: tall, blonde, suntanned. There was nothing gawky about her freckles. They blended into her honey complexion. She was exactly the way I had imagined the all-American girl. She was wearing shorts like a cheerleader. I had to force my eyes up from her long, shapely legs. They glowed. She wasn't just Carrie Morrison. She was the America of TV and the movies. She was a whole other world.

'I play soccer,' Carrie told me.

I was trying not to stand on my tongue.

'What position?'

There was a twinkle in her eyes.

'Usually next to the ball.'

'No, I mean—'

'I know what you mean,' she said.

She flicked her cheerleader hair and gave a cheerleader smile. Not just her lips. Her eyes smiled too. They were a startling light blue, like the sky at the start of *The Simpsons*. I read a poem at school once. What was that colour?

'Azure,' I murmured.

'What?'

'Oh nothing. Thinking out loud, that's all.'

'Do you always think about colours?'

I thought she was teasing, but I didn't care. She could tease me all she liked. If Heaven was a person, it would look like her. I listened to the music coming out of the open kitchen door and the spit of the meat on the grill and the sounds of the warm evening and I felt like the luckiest guy in the world.

I wanted to stay lucky for ever.

Next morning I met up with the rest of the team for a training session. We stood awkwardly in our new surroundings with the sun on our faces and stories of our temporary homes on our lips.

'You should see their car. They've got this massive SUV.'

'Listen to him. He's got the lingo already.'

'What's SUV stand for anyway?'

'Straight up vehicle?'

'Don't be stupid!'

'They've got a kitchen the size of my whole house. You should see it. I ate my cereal really carefully so I didn't splash the counter.'

'Hear that? America must be something if it can teach him manners! They do have paper towels, you know.'

Everybody laughed.

'Yes, I find myself tiptoeing round the place like it's some kind of museum or library or something.'

'I know what you mean,' Kyle said. 'I folded my dirty washing this morning!'

'That's stupid. What do you want to fold dirty washing for?'

'I don't know. It just felt wrong screwing it up and leaving it on the floor like I do at home.'

Some had more pressing concerns than dirty washing.

'The daughter in my place is *fit*.'

I found myself thinking of my own fit girl. There were girls I liked back home. But I saw them every day in their blue skirts and jumpers, ankle socks and soft-soled shoes. I saw them wrapped in jackets against the wind with their hair blown across their faces. They were real girls with real flaws. The girls back home weren't naturally tanned and golden. The orange ones went to the tanning salon or sprayed themselves bronze. Everybody had a similar tale to tell.

Of spacious houses. Impressive cars. Fit girls.

Excitement crackled around the group.

Mick put us through our paces. He watched us chasing across the turf, passing, moving, finding space. After the gluey tug of wintry English soil, the dry, firm pitch was a surprise. I sprinted to recover one mishit ball and paused to gaze at the morning sun.

'Some place, isn't it?' Mick asked.

'Amazing.'

'How are you getting on with the Morrisons?'

'Great. Yes, no problems.'

'He's a key man over here, Mr Morrison. None of this would have happened without him.'

I took advantage of a poor back pass, lobbed the keeper and strode away with my arms in the air, head thrown back to bask in the adulation. There wasn't any, but I enjoyed the moment. Mick glanced at the ball nestling in the net and scowled. He didn't like me showboating. He called us together.

'Think you can do that against our first opponents, Ethan?'

'What's stopping me?'

'The All Stars. I watched a video of them. They're a local side.'

One of the boys scoffed.

'Yanks? Football's a girl's game over here. The boys play American football. That's rugby with helmets and guards shoved under their shirts.'

'If you lads want to take a trophy home,' Mick told us, 'you're going to have to be on top of your game. The ground's firmer than you're used to. The game will be fast and it's going to be hot on that pitch. You'll have to pace yourselves and take your opportunities. Drop your game and you've let the club down. Got it?'

We didn't get it. The first half was a nightmare. Mick started the half-time team talk. Our shoulders slumped.

Our heads were down. We were losing. Against kids from a country where football was a girl's game.

'You did it your way.' Mick leaned forward to press the point home. 'You were lazy and arrogant. You went out there showing off, running around like eleven headless chickens. Now we do it my way. I'm going to see hard work, *teamwork*. You're going to close them down, work for each other, give these boys some respect ... and beat them.'

I squinted against the sunlight, picking out Carrie. She was chatting to some of the All Star boys. I felt a tug of jealousy.

The All Stars dominated the first ten minutes then Kyle cleared it. Jack came in from the wing to collect the ball. Running onto the pass he hit it first time. It skimmed across the turf right into my path. It was easy to side-foot it under the keeper's despairing dive. I didn't have to wait for the net to bulge. I'd just given the All Stars something to think about. Squeaky bum time.

I peeled away. I passed Mick on the touchline, but it was Carrie I was looking for. I met the sky blue eyes and smiled. She smiled back. That was the turning point in the game. Jack got the equaliser. Kyle headed in the third from a corner. I made the result safe with a stoppage-time penalty. I stripped off my shirt and stood swigging from a water bottle. The sun stung my shoulders.

'You want to put sunblock on that pale British skin,' Carrie told me. She pronounced it Briddish. She put long fingers on the top of my back. It felt good. The sun had stung me. Her touch burned me.

I phoned Mum that night.

'Yes, I'm good. We won 4-2. We had to come back from two down.'

'Did you score?'

I tried to sound offhand, so I didn't come across big-headed. I promised to ring again in a couple of days and hung up. I stared at the phone for a while then I went to see what Carrie was doing. Somehow, I couldn't shift the frown from my face or the doubts from my mind.

It was the way Mum kept saying everything was fine.

Like it wasn't.

The Zero Gravity Thrill Park did what it said on the tin. Carrie was my partner on the two-person ride. She was scared out of her skin.

'You sure about this?'

Her face was pinched and tense, her vivid blue eyes wide and uncertain.

'I'll be fine.'

That word again. Suddenly everybody was fine. Mum was fine. Alex and Declan were fine. Now Carrie. Texas Blastoff was a giant, two-seater slingshot. We were rocking gently a few metres above the ground. I smiled as she checked her harness for the third time. I let my gaze move over her legs. She was wearing shorts again. She looked good in them. She knew it too.

'Ready?'

'Uh huh.' She gave me a heart-stopping smile that trembled on her lips then fell away. 'I just wish they'd get on with iiiiiiiittttt!'

The final word was a piercing scream as the ride blasted us fifty metres into the air, zero to seventy in little over a second. We fizzed into the sky then we were tumbling, twisting, rolling, flipping. In the rush of air I heard Carrie shrieking.

She planted a kiss on my cheek.

'What's that for?' I whispered.

'Being you,' she answered.

I nodded.

'I'm good at that.'

The Green seemed a million miles away.

We won our match against the Canadians and against a Juventus team. We would be playing Chivas Guadalajara in the final. Chivas were good, better even than the All Stars. They were fast, skilful, professional if that's the right word to use about fourteen-year-old boys, but the team had started listening to Mick so we were holding them 0-0. Halfway through the first half the central defender marking me kicked the back of my calf. I felt the sharp jab of pain. I reacted, shoving an elbow in his face. I was lucky to get away with a few harsh words from the ref. I knew I was in for a rollocking during the interval.

'What was that about, Ethan?' Mick asked. 'I thought you'd got that kind of thing out of your system.'

I saw Kyle watching. He hadn't forgotten the time I nearly broke his ankle.

'Didn't you see what he did? He ran his studs down my leg.'

'I know what *he* did. It's what you did that matters. You don't react. End of.'

I went to protest.

'End of! The ref was blindsided. He missed the incident completely. You could have got yourself sent off. You owe it to your teammates to show some self-discipline.'

'Easy for you to say. You haven't got somebody kicking lumps out of you.'

'*I* don't want a career in Premiership football.'

Chivas came back strongly and equalised ten minutes later. After that the Mexicans pressed hard for the winner. Just when it looked as if it was going to come, Kyle cleared the ball upfield. I gathered it with the instep of my right foot and pushed it past the defender. I was one on one with the keeper. I chipped it and watched with satisfaction as it rolled into the net. I glimpsed Carrie standing behind the goal and frowned. A tall, dark-haired boy had his arm round her waist when I scored. She squirmed free and started jumping up and down, applauding wildly. Kyle lifted the trophy as team captain. The biggest roar was when I took it from him. The tannoy announced that I was man of the match.

I sat next to Carrie on the way back.

'So you've got a boyfriend?' I asked.

'Well, kind of,' she said.

Kind of. Maybe I had a chance.

Kind of.

What do you do on your last evening in another world?

You try to make it special.

I didn't know what to make of Carrie. She blew hot and cold. Sometimes she was intimate, inviting, so warm she made me feel like the most special person on earth. Other times she was this ice queen, a splinter of aloofness who left me feeling spurned and foolish. Which was the real Carrie? I didn't know how I was supposed to find out and there was no time to take it slow. I was in new territory. I didn't know the rules of this game.

I packed my suitcase. At least, I shoved everything I had inside it. I stood there willing her to wander in and exchange small talk. Hadn't I seen her hopping up and down, applauding my success in the tournament? Didn't that mean something? But she didn't give me a second glance. She sat all the way across the living room tapping away at the computer. She was on Facebook. From time to time she would sit back in her chair and shout a comment to her parents or her little sister. She didn't once draw me into the conversation. Maybe this was the real meaning of loneliness. Being in a room with somebody you're crazy about and she doesn't know you exist.

Then there she was, leaning over my shoulder. She wrapped her arms round me.

'I'll miss you,' she said.

On impulse, I pulled her close and pressed my lips against hers. She darted backwards, eyelids fluttering, a nervous giggle escaping from her lips.

'I'll stay in touch,' I promised. 'I'll friend you on Facebook.'

I didn't get to see her again.

Ever.

7

Then home. Then pain.

'You OK?'

Alex was doing the asking. I nodded, feeling stupid for taking it so badly. I was lying on my back on the bed, staring up at the ceiling. I didn't speak. Couldn't speak. For the shortest time life had been full. Then I came home and Declan had gone.

'It can't have come as a surprise.' Alex shut the door with a back-kick. 'He never stays long.'

I fought for the words.

'Doesn't make it any easier. He promised. He said it was different this time.' I blew out my cheeks out and rubbed my eyes to stop tears that didn't quite come. 'Look at me. I pretended it didn't matter. I swore he'd never get to me. You were right that time. I'm pathetic, you know that?'

I could feel the weight of Alex's silence.

'If Declan could see me now, he'd be laughing himself sick. All those years, all the betrayals and he still had me believing in him. I must be really stupid.'

'You wanted a dad. We're all the same.'

'Even you? You never made your peace with him.'

Alex pulled a face. 'I was ready to. If he'd stayed another couple of weeks I might even have started calling him Dad.'

I gave an incredulous laugh. 'No way!'

'Stranger things have happened. Everybody's looking for a miracle.'

We sat there in silence. Finally I thought about somebody other than myself. 'So how's Mum?'

'Pretty low. This is the longest he's ever stuck around since we were little. She thought he'd finally got his head sorted. He even nicked fifty quid off her.' He ran his palm over his scalp. 'Let's change the subject, eh? How was America?'

'Good. Yes, really good.'

It was the man-thing, I suppose. You talk football because you don't have a language for the things that really matter.

'We played some top sides.'

'And you beat the lot?'

'We brought the trophy home, didn't we?' I had something I wanted to share. 'There was a girl.'

'Yes? Well, let's have the details, you dirty dog.'

I smiled as if I had something to smile about.

'Her name's Carrie.'

'Cute?'

'Gorgeous. Man, she glowed. I wish I could have stayed longer.'

'Got a photo?'

'No and I wouldn't show you if I did. I don't want my letch of a brother slobbering over her.'

'You don't need to worry on that score. I've met somebody myself.'

'You have! When did this happen?'

'While you were away.'

'Bet she's a dog.'

He took a swipe at me. 'Watch it.'

'What's her name?'

'Lindsay.'

I saw a blonde two years above me at school. Something told me she'd left to work in a shop.

'Lindsay Clarke?'

'That's her. Got something to say?'

'No, she's fit. She's no Carrie, though.'

That's how we were, always riding each other. We did it even when we were getting along.

It was a week before I got the longed-for email from America.

I opened it excitedly, but it was from Mr Morrison, not Carrie. It thanked me for being such a good guest, no trouble at all. I thought I might print it off and show Mick and Eddie. See, I can behave myself. I kept reading, hoping for some mention of Carrie. When it came it was a big disappointment.

'You were a great hit with Carrie,' Mr Morrison wrote. 'She said it was like having a brother around the place again.'

A *brother*!

Was that it? The kiss. The way she grabbed my hand. That was about being some kind of brother and sister? That was about being *friends*? Stuff that. I shoved my chair back and snorted. Alex was passing.

'What's up with you?'

'Carrie,' I said. 'She says I'm like a brother.'

Alex burst out laughing.

'A brother! Now that can't be good. Is that it then, your great romance? You wind up just good friends?'

'Yes, that's it,' I answered mournfully. 'I thought …'

'Well, looks like you thought wrong.'

Mr Morrison had sent some jpegs of photos he had taken. I opened them one by one. In the final photo Carrie was in the background. The boyfriend was there, the guy I had seen at the last match. He had his arms round her waist, lips hovering close to her neck. I deleted the email. That was one set of photos I wasn't going to keep. What an idiot I'd been.

Me and Carrie?

Dream on.

The gun didn't go away.

A month after they put Jamie away there were police cars outside the Leathers' house. They lived at the back of us and I saw the rippling blue lights against my bedroom curtains. It happened in the early hours one Sunday morning.

Neighbours gathered on the street corner next day. It was a warm spring dawn so some of the men were bare-chested and smoking. I heard people talking. One man said what everybody else was thinking.

'Somebody shot out their living room window.' Then, as an afterthought, he added, 'Pity they weren't downstairs at the time.'

He realised what he'd said and shifted his feet uncomfortably. On the Green you never knew who was listening. Badmouth the gangs and your name would go up on walls or maybe your house got a visit.

I imagined the dull punch of the bullet that came through the Leathers' window, the shower of broken glass. I saw Alex's face out of the corner of my eye. It was white and pinched. He returned to the house. Mum was chatting to a woman from down the street. She tried to say something to Alex, but he brushed past her and went inside. I exchanged glances with Mum and followed him. I shoved the door to and asked my question.

'This is down to the NSC, right?'

'Who else?'

'Do you think they were after Dean, you know, take out Jamie's second in command?'

Alex shook his head.

'It happened about three o'clock this morning, a time when everybody's going to be in bed. The house was in darkness. It was a warning, that's all. Carl Nash was sending a calling card, telling Jamie he's lost the war.'

'Do you think Jamie will listen?'

'Have you lost your marbles? There's nothing Jamie can do while he's inside, but he won't let this go. No way. He'll bide his time, but the moment he's out he'll go after Carl.'

'The way things are going, Jamie won't have any soldiers left.'

'You don't know Jamie. If anybody can come back from the dead, he can.'

Alarm bells rang.

'You're not part of this, are you?'

Alex looked at me as if I had crawled out from under a rock.

'Are you stupid? I'm done with all that. I've got a job. I've got a girlfriend. I don't need the Tribe.'

The front door slammed. Mum appeared.

'Don't say it, OK?' Alex growled. 'Ethan's just been giving me the third degree. I don't need you to start. This is Jamie's business. It's got nothing to do with me.'

'You sure?'

'I'm sure.'

Mitch showed up a few hours later.

'I heard about the shooting.' He was breathless with excitement. He was a scavenger of the plain: he came running at the scent of blood. 'Anybody hurt?'

I told him no. He looked disappointed.

'They took out a window.'

Mitch nodded. Still disappointed. A window. Not somebody's head.

'There's somebody boarding it up.'

'So why'd you ask?'

'I just thought there might be more to it.'

I grabbed my jacket and headed for the door.

'Where're you going?' Mitch asked.

'To see somebody. You coming?'

'Why not?' Mitch said. 'I've nothing else to do.'

He asked a question with his eyes, but I wasn't talking. Mitch understood when we turned into the street where Sean Tennant lived.

'We're going to see Sean?'

'That's right.'

'What for?'

'I need to know if there's more to this than Alex is saying.'

'Alex won't like it. Sean's his mate, not yours.'

I pressed the doorbell. 'I don't care.'

Mrs Tennant answered and shouted to Sean. Mitch saw the bruises on his face at the same time as me. We swapped glances. Sean closed the door behind him so nobody could hear.

'Did Alex send you?'

I didn't answer. I wanted to know about the bruises.

'Before I say, tell me about your face. Walk into a door?'

Sean looked uncomfortable.

'It was Carl Nash, wasn't it?'

'Keep your voice down. I fed my old lady a line, but she's still suspicious.'

'So what happened?'

'NSC happened. They're going round everybody involved in the Tribe. Seems they're calling on us one by one. Dean had better have something up his sleeve. People are bricking it.'

'Don't you know about last night?'

Sean's eyes said he didn't.

'Somebody shot up Jamie's house.'

Sean cursed.

'Anybody hurt?'

'Just the window. I'd say Dean's going to be lying low, wouldn't you? Jamie's name's gone toxic.'

'That why you came, Ethan? You wanted to tell me about the drive by?'

'Alex doesn't know anything about this. I'm doing it for Mum. I need to know if Alex is finished with the Tribe. I've got to be certain this isn't going to drag him back in.'

'You're worried about him?'

'I'm worried what it might do to Mum.'

Sean folded his arms.

'What do you want me to do, Ethan, take a lie detector test? If I wasn't finished with Jamie Leather and his crew before the shooting, I am now. Same goes for Alex.'

That was good enough for me. I slapped Mitch's arm.

'Come on, we're done here.'

We walked away.

'Do you believe him?' Mitch asked.

I nodded.

'He's got no reason to lie to me. The Tribe are finished. The Green belongs to NSC now.'

8

Mick leaned against the minibus. The bonnet was open.

'Sorry boys, we're not going anywhere.'

There were rolled eyes all round.

'So what do we do, Mick?'

'I'll make a few phone calls,' Mick said. 'Some of your parents are insured to take you in their cars. I'm sure Eddie will chip in.'

I'd been wondering about Eddie. It wasn't like him to miss a game.

'Where is Eddie anyway?'

'Said he felt a bit under the weather.' Mick glanced at his watch. 'You won't have to hang around for long. It's only a twenty-mile drive. We'll be on the move in three quarters of an hour, an hour at most.'

He started making calls. The other lads wandered back to the changing rooms. It was raining steadily. I stayed outside, staring up at the hills. They were grey under the clouds, then the sun came out and turned them shades of jade and emerald.

'What are you standing there for?' Jack asked. 'You're getting soaked.'

There must have been something in the way I looked at him because he went quiet.

'I'm only saying.'

'I like the fresh air,' I told him. 'I like looking at the hills.'

Jack followed the direction of his stare.

'What's so great about hills?'

'They're wild. Don't you ever get sick of seeing nothing but houses?'

Jack thought.

'Not really. Why do you like wild things?'

One of the other boys walked past. 'He is a wild thing.'

I wandered to the far end of the training ground, leaving him behind. The opposition players were getting into their parents' cars. Some eyed me with curiosity. I'd scored a hat trick on the way to a 4-2 away victory. I knew what they were saying.

He's good.

They say he's going to make it in the Premiership.

Yes, remember the name.

My name was coming up on some hardcore fans' radar as a future prospect. I was getting mentions in the junior football supplement in the local paper. Suddenly the dream was taking on solid form. Some nights I would lie in bed whispering: *I can make it.* The rain continued to patter on my shoulders and drip off my eyebrows. It was a long way from Dallas. I thought about Carrie. It was getting hard to imagine her face. A seagull hung on the wind for a few moments then flapped away over the rooftops and out of sight. A fierce sun burned the clouds and a rainbow arced in the middle distance. Mick wasn't looking. He was more interested in getting us home.

'Gather round, lads,' he shouted.

I left the rainbow behind and joined the cluster of boys.

'I've organised lifts for everybody. There's a café just down the road. It's a bit of a greasy spoon, but you can get toast and a drink. I'll stand the cost.'

Kyle laughed.

'So it's full English breakfasts all round then?'

'You wish.'

The café was warm. The piles of toast were welcome. I got the window table.

'Is it true somebody got shot in your road?' Jack asked.

I kept my eyes on the street.

'What do you want to ask that for?'

'My dad saw it in the paper. So is it?'

'It was a window. Nobody got hurt.'

'What was it about?' Kyle asked. 'Drugs?'

'No.' My face burned. Was I ever going to escape coming from the Green? 'Why's it got to be about drugs? It was just a frightener, all right? It's not that big a deal.'

Kyle thought that was funny.

'Gunfire's not that big a deal? Joking, aren't you? It must be rough where you live.'

'It is,' Jack said. 'Don't you know what the Green's like?'

I tried to put him straight.

'It's no different to anywhere else.'

Who was I kidding? They both lived on new estates with show houses on the corner. Their fathers always pulled up in new cars. They had good jobs. There weren't many men working on Bevan Way. There weren't many

95

men, full stop. It was the women who brought in the money, women like Mum. They kept things together.

'Not much different!' Jack scoffed.

'It isn't,' I insisted.

'My dad calls it Benefits Green. He says they should cut people's payments and make them work for a living.'

I leaned forward, laying my fists on the table.

'What does he know? My mum's got a job.'

They both watched my fists. They only half took the hint.

'What does she do?'

There was a moment's hesitation.

'She works in the dry cleaners.'

I gave Jack a stare, a warning not to say another word. At that moment Mick came over.

'Good to see you lads getting along,' he said. 'The first lifts are here.'

It was a couple of parents. Jack's dad was one of them. I watched the café empty.

'There's space in our car,' Jack said.

I swigged my Coke.

'It's OK. I'll wait for Eddie. He won't like it if he drives all this way and there's nobody here.'

That wasn't the reason. I didn't want to sit there, hearing how great their lives were. Eddie arrived ten minutes later. He sat down and dabbed his face with a handkerchief. He didn't look too good.

'You all right, Eddie? You're sweating.'

'I woke up with a bit of a bug this morning. I've been feeling sick. That's why I cried off.'

'You OK to drive?'

'It's just a funny stomach. I'll be fine.'

I didn't give it much thought, but it was the first sign something was wrong.

Eddie hunched over the steering wheel. His eyes were hard, lips pinched. It didn't look like concentration. It was pain.

'You sure you're all right, Ed?'

'Yes, I must have eaten something. My system's haywire.' He blinked back the discomfort and changed the subject. 'Mick's been singing your praises this week.'

Suddenly I wasn't thinking about Eddie.

'For real?'

'He's very impressed by your play in the States. He liked the way you worked for the team.'

'It was a matter of having to.'

I do a good line in false modesty.

'Yes, well the point is you did it, son.'

Then he wheezed. His face was glazed with sweat.

'You don't look good, Ed. Do you want to pull over?'

This time he didn't answer at all. The only sound was the beat of the windscreen wipers and the hiss of the tyres on the road.

'Eddie? … Ed?'

He groaned and grabbed for his chest. His hands slipped off the steering wheel. I lunged for it as the vehicle lurched into the oncoming traffic. Headlights flashed a blinding glow across the windscreen.

'Eddie!'

He fought to control the car then rocked back, eyes squeezed shut in agony. There was the blare of a horn, more headlights then we clipped a white van and spun off the road. The tyres shrieked. The engine roared. We were rolling over and over, metal howling and buckling. It was as if somebody was pounding on the car with giant fists. The world swirled and crashed around us. The terrifying thumping and crunching seemed to go on for ever then the vehicle came to a halt.

It was a few moments before I was able to clear my senses. Eddie was lying very still next to me, a smear of blood on his forehead, incoherent words bubbling on his lips. I tried to get to him, but something was pinning me down. I had an air bag against my chest, but that wasn't what was bothering me. I had this weight crushing my knee. An invisible hand was trying to twist my kneecap right out of my leg. I struggled to control the pain then forced out a few words.

'Eddie, can you hear me? We've got to get out of here. Ed, I'm scared. It's my leg. It's crushed.'

That's when I realised how bad he was. His skin was grey. My leg was getting worse. I tried to shift my weight to ease it. Why didn't somebody help? I yelled at the top of my voice.

'Help. Help me!'

There had been a white van. There was other traffic too. They all saw what happened. Where were they? They must have stopped. Why didn't they come?

'Help me someone!'

Pain ripped through Eddie again. His chest rose then he lay still. I carried on yelling for help, but no one came. No matter how I tried to ease the pressure on my knee, nothing helped. Beside me, Eddie was ominously still.

My mobile. Where was my mobile? I groped around desperately. It was over to my left, just out of reach. I strained after it, but I couldn't get to it. Gritting my teeth, I tore my knee free from the twisted metal. To my horror, I felt something pop. It was a sickening sensation. The pain was so bad tears came. I blinked them away and phoned 999.

'You've got to help me. Please. It's Eddie. He's in a bad way.'

The operator tried to calm me down. With her help I managed to mumble out the details of the crash. She asked where I was.

'I don't know.'

'Can you see any road signs?'

I crawled out of the vehicle. Pain was clawing around my knee. There was something about the feel of it that scared me. People were coming, two men and a woman, running along the side of the road.

'Where are we?' I yelled. 'Where the hell are we?'

The woman took the phone and gave the operator the information she needed. The men were leaning into the wreck of the car.

'Tell them to get a move on. The driver doesn't look good.'

I lay on my back with the rain beating on my face. Soon the revolving blue lights of the ambulance and the fire engine were washing the scene. Now that Eddie was getting help, I was starting to wonder about the state of my knee. How much of the season was I going to miss? I was sobbing. I don't know if it was for Eddie, or for me.

Eddie was sitting up in his hospital bed.

He looked tired. His face still had that grey look, but he was alive.

'What did they do to you, Eddie?'

'They put a stent in.'

'Come again?'

Eddie looked pained, as if it was too much effort to talk. His wife Eileen took over.

'They inserted a catheter – a kind of tube – through the femoral artery in his groin. They push this little stent thing, a thin tube, into his coronary artery.'

It sounded like torture.

'They put it in his heart, you mean and they did it through his …?'

'Yes, it keeps the artery open.'

I couldn't get the idea out of my head, shoving something right through your body.

'They stuck something in your heart?'

'If they hadn't I'd have popped my clogs.'

'You gave me one hell of a scare, Ed.'

Eddie managed something like a chuckle.

'Gave myself one, son.'

'You should never have got in that car, you stupid old goat,' Eileen said. 'You knew you weren't feeling right.'

He tapped her arm and whispered something. Eileen turned to me.

'He wants to know about your knee.'

I'd been trying to avoid any discussion of my leg. I patted my crutches, kind of casually.

'I'll be playing again before you know it.'

Eddie's taut features relaxed.

'You're the best young player I've ever seen. I hope you haven't done yourself any permanent damage.'

I lied about my knee.

'No, a bit of bruising, that's all.'

His eyelids were drooping.

'I think it's time to let him sleep,' Eileen said.

I started to swing away on my crutches.

'Ethan,' Eddie croaked. 'Ethan!'

'Yes.'

'You probably saved my life.'

Eileen accompanied me down the corridor. There was a question in her pale eyes.

'You weren't being completely honest with Eddie, were you?'

My heart kicked.

'What do you mean?'

'You know what I mean, Ethan.'

'I pulled it a bit, that's all.'

'You risked your football career to help my Eddie.' She watched my face. 'You can be honest with me, Ethan. How bad is it?'

I went through a strange moment of hurt and relief.

'They don't know for sure. I felt something go.'

'Oh, Ethan.'

I swallowed hard. I wasn't going to say anything in front of Eddie. I didn't want him feeling guilty. The consultant had said something about major ligament damage. They were going to operate in two weeks. I knew what that meant. Players with cruciate ligament injuries were out for six months.

Maybe longer.

And I had more than one problem. There was damage to the bones in the joint.

'Don't say anything to Eddie,' I pleaded. 'You know what he's like. He'll only feel responsible.'

Eileen squeezed my shoulder.

'You can rely on me.'

Mum was waiting with a taxi at the main entrance. I watched the city speed by. Six months out. It felt like a prison sentence.

But it wasn't six months. The operation was the beginning of a year-long nightmare. First there was the blood clot. They did something called aspirating. They pulled the clot out with a needle. Then there was the infection. They tried antibiotics. The infection went away for a while, but it came back. The problems went on month after month. I prayed for an end to it. I just wanted to know if I was ever going to play again. But there was no end. There was an operation to clear up bone fragments in my knee. It never felt right. It was as if I was stumbling along a swaying tightrope. The tightrope was my one chance of playing again and all around it was a horrible, aching void. It went on and on.

Mum and Alex were true as steel. We were a family. Alex had his apprenticeship and he had his girl. If anything, he was stronger than Mum. She did her best, but she found it hard to look at me without her eyes filling with tears. She knew how much football meant to me. She sensed the black emptiness all around me if my football career was over.

And the gun was always there. Mitch seemed to know everything that happened on the street. Jamie's granddad died a few months later and they let him out for the day of the funeral. He was in the car that followed the hearse. A dozen NSC turned up, six on each side of the road. Call it a guard of dishonour. They waited for Jamie to arrive. The moment they saw him they made the shape of a gun with fingers and thumb. Their outstretched arms followed him all the way into the crematorium. They did it in silence. You would have thought Jamie would be cowed. Not a bit of it. He pulled free of his minders just for a moment and shouted his defiance. He puffed out his chest and he faced the outstretched arms and the pointing fingers. He shouted and they stood in silence. The war between the Tribe and NSC was an unwatered seed, buried deep, but it wasn't dead.

Months later I was sitting with Mum in the consultant's office.

'So what's the score, Doc?'

I sat forward in my seat, willing Dr Hart to give me some good news. He said a lot about ligaments, anterior and cruciate. He talked about the alignment of the knee. I'd heard it all before. All I wanted was the pay off. All I wanted was a chance.

'What does all that mean?'

'You must have considered this option, Ethan,' Dr Hart said. 'I'm not going to give you false hope.'

I saw the look of sympathy in Mum's eyes. No false hope. Simply put, that meant no hope at all.

'You did serious damage to the knee in the accident,' Dr Hart said. 'We're not talking about a single problem. I wish we were.'

'What are you saying?' I asked. 'Am I going to play again?'

'You can't rule anything out definitively, but I would say it is very, very unlikely.'

The tightrope had just snapped. I was falling into empty space and there was no end to the fall, no bottom to my despair.

'But there's still a chance? People come back from knee injuries.'

'There is a chance, yes, but a very small one, I'm afraid. This isn't a single injury, Ethan, and it isn't just muscular.'

I waited for something, anything positive. It didn't come.

'If I were you, I would face the possibility that you won't play competitive football again. I have sent the club a full report.'

I couldn't hear for the roar of blood in my ears. I couldn't speak. Mum put the question for me.

'Just tell us straight, doctor. If you had to give a one-word answer, will he play again, yes or no, which would it be?'

Dr Hart tried to avoid the question.

I managed a single word.

'Please.'

Dr Hart looked me in the eye.

'No.'

PART TWO

THE YEAR OF FIRE

9

Jamie did less than eighteen months. A lot can happen in that time, but some things never change. The gun was still there. It was waiting for Jamie Leather when he came out of prison. It was raining the day he walked through the gates. Dean and Jason were waiting for him outside, their shoulders dark with damp. The brothers embraced.

'Good to have you back, bro,' Dean said.

'Good to be back,' Jamie answered. 'Let's go and see Mum.'

I was coming home from school when the car went past us and took the next left. Mitch nudged me.

'That's Jamie Leather. I told you he was coming home.'

Mitch worried me. I stayed away from Dean and Jason, Jamie's youngest ugliest brother. Not Mitch. He liked being seen with them. He seemed to know everything that was going down on the Green. You didn't have to be a mind-reader to know where he got his information. We used to be inseparable. Lately, he would vanish without a word. Jamie got out of the car.

'Do you think he's changed?'

Even as I said it, I knew it was wishful thinking. We stood at the corner of Jamie's street and watched the brothers standing by the car, making sure everybody saw them. Blinds and curtains twitched. Jamie saw Mitch and me and acknowledged us briefly. Mitch nodded back. I blanked Jamie. It seemed to amuse him.

'Don't make him an enemy,' Mitch advised.

'Don't tell me what to do, Mitch. I can make my own decisions.'

'Just make the right ones. You could get yourself hurt.'

I frowned. 'That sounds like some kind of threat, Mitch. What's wrong with you lately?'

He shrugged. 'The Green's a tough place. Get tough or get trodden on. Just the way it is.'

Jamie closed the door and I stood in the rain imagining the scene inside. He would have eaten, listened to his mother's stories and showered. He wouldn't hang around long. He had things to do.

I was able to piece the story together later with Mitch's help. Jamie sat in the car while Dean walked down the row of deserted industrial units, forced up the roller doors and retrieved the Walther pistol from the steel shelving where it had lain since he went down. Dean handed Jamie the gun. Jamie examined it then shoved it in the glove compartment.

'A bit of a clean and it's good to go.'

'When are you going to do it?' Dean asked.

'There's no hurry,' Jamie said. 'We wait for our moment.'

*

Alex got his news a couple of weeks after Jamie walked free from prison. The front door slammed and he went straight upstairs. Mum came in from the kitchen. It was as if a shadow had blurred by, bringing cold into the house.

'Was that Alex?'

'Yes.'

Something was wrong.

'Ask him what he wants for his tea.'

I had just reached the bottom of the stairs when Alex came rushing towards me, shrugging his jacket over his shoulders. He had a wild look on his face.

'Are you OK?'

There wasn't even a pause before he answered.

'No, I'm not all right.'

His voice came out low and hollow.

'What is it?'

'A piece of advice, Ethan. Expect nothing from this world and you'll never be disappointed, because that's what we get: nothing.'

'What are you talking about?'

'Life's a crock, bro. You used to be a footballer. I used to be a plumber. Now we're nothing, either of us.'

Mum had heard. She joined us in the hall.

'*Used* to be a plumber? Oh Alex, what's happened?'

He was fumbling for his phone, keen to be somewhere else.

'Remember how I told you the work's been drying up. They had to let some people go. Sean and I were last in. That means we're first out. We're expendable.'

None of us knew how much Alex needed that job until the day he lost it. In the weeks to come all the life would go out of him. But life doesn't allow empty spaces. Something malignant would grow in the void left by the discipline of the working day. That Friday afternoon was just the beginning.

Mum put her hand on his arm. 'What are you going to do?'

Alex stared ahead. He was unresponsive. Anger flared, then fell away. 'I suppose I'll sign on. Look for another job.' He leaned against the wall. 'I'm not holding out much hope. There's nothing out there.'

'You can't start with that attitude.'

'I'm not starting with any attitude,' Alex said. 'I've just had my guts kicked out. I'm not in any mood for reassurance. 'Then he groaned, as if remembering something he would rather forget. 'The timing's brilliant. I've just booked that holiday for Lindsay and me.'

'You'll have to cancel it.'

'No way! I promised her.'

Mum gave a sympathetic smile. 'You can't spend every penny you have on a holiday. She'll understand.'

I wasn't so sure. The times I'd met Lindsay, I'd got a picture of somebody who liked her creature comforts. She wasn't the kind who was going to hang around out of loyalty.

Alex pushed himself off the wall. 'I'm going to see her, break the bad news about my job.'

Mum tugged at the blinds and watched him walking down the road. He had a weight on his shoulders.

'He loved that job. Worked hard at it. I feel so sorry for him. I hope he gets something soon. Alex needs something to fill his days. You know what he's like when he's got time on his hands.' She didn't need to spell it out.

We both remembered what he'd been like before Jamie vanished off the scene. She saw the time. 'You'd better get ready. Eddie will be round soon.'

Eddie had arranged for me to get a second opinion on my knee. I was also going to have some physio.

'Don't build your hopes up,' she said.

'I'm not, but I've got to give it a go, Mum. Football's the only thing I ever wanted to do.'

'I know. Just remember what the consultant said. You know I want the best for you. It would be lovely if you got to play again, but be realistic, son, that's all.'

'Don't worry,' I told her. 'I know it's an outside chance.'

It didn't stop me chasing daydreams. Eddie arrived five minutes later and we drove to the top of the road and hung a left. I saw something and twisted round.

'Just pull in here a second, Eddie.'

We waited for a moment with the engine idling.

'What is it?'

Jamie's Subaru was parked outside the Beehive pub. There was a crowd of boys gathered round it. One of them was Mitch. Alex was there too. He had his head through the car window. The skin on the back of my neck prickled.

'I thought it was somebody I knew.'

'Was it?'

Sometimes lies are easier than the truth.

'No, I made a mistake. Drive on.'

'So what do you think? Will the physio help?'

Eddie and I were standing side by side, leaning on the railings, watching the five-a-side. It was tough seeing Mick put lads I knew like Jack and Kyle through their paces. They were progressing through the Academy. Jack in particular seemed to be going places. I gave Eddie a non-committal answer.

'It's going to take time, Ed.'

'We can go if you're ready.'

That's what made Eddie the best. He could read minds. He was where I was, kicking every ball. I itched to get out on the pitch, create space, hear the ball snap against the net like I did in Dallas. I wasn't kidding myself. It was going to be a long time, if ever.

'Don't worry about me, Ed,' I told him. 'I can handle it.'

'I've heard that before, son. It's hard to let go of a dream.'

'If the physios do their magic, I won't need to.'

My reply struck a false note. I knew it. He knew it. We were about to go when Mick blew the whistle. Instantly, the boys sprinted towards me.

'How are you doing, Ethan?'

'Yes, how's the knee?'

'When are you coming back?'

I did what was expected of me, told the guys what they wanted to hear.

'I'm getting treatment. You watch your place, Jack. I'm on the way back.'

'Good to hear it, Ethan. We miss that bad temper of yours.'

Kyle put on a theatrical grimace. 'Like hell.'

Eddie glanced at his watch. 'We've got to be going, boys.'

I walked away through the goodbyes and the good lucks. Mick jogged after us and added a quiet word out of the hearing of the team.

'Whatever happens, Ethan, the club's here for you. Don't forget it.'

'Thanks Mick.'

By the time we got to the car Mick was putting the boys through their warm down. I paused before getting in, watching the scene.

'Do you think I'll ever be out there with them, Ed?

'You tell me, son. I gave up mind-reading when they took my crystal ball off me.'

'I'm going to do it, Ed.'

'Good to hear it. Like Mick says, we'll give you every bit of support we can.'

We drove back to the Green in silence. The city streets shuffled by. They were meaner and smaller than I remembered them before the accident. It was as if the edges of the world were flaking, crumbling away. Everything was diminished. I stopped Eddie before we got to Bevan.

'Drop me here. I'm going to call on Mitch.'

I had business to discuss. There was no answer at the house so I called him.

'Yes?'

'We need to talk.'

'Sounds heavy. What's bothering you?'

'Face to face, Mitch.'

There was a moment's silence.

'Fine. See you outside the 24/7. Ten minutes.'

I was early. He was late. He was sporting a brand new, spotless pair of trainers.

'Did your Lotto numbers come up?' I asked, nodding at the shoes.

He didn't offer an explanation for the smart new

trainers. I let it slide. I had more important things to ask.

'I saw you earlier. You were talking to Jamie.'

'It's a free country.'

'Alex was there'

'Who's arguing? What's eating you, Ethan?'

I didn't like the new Mitch. There was a time we told each other everything. Now he had secrets.

'Alex swore he was going to stay away from the Tribe. He promised Mum.'

Mitch jangled the change in his pocket.

'I'm getting a Coke. You want one?'

'I want answers first. We're mates, Mitch. When did we start keeping things from each other?'

He treated me to a cool stare.

'Don't look at me, Ethan. Jamie called me over. If he wants to talk to you, you don't ignore him.'

'And Alex?'

Mitch shrugged.

'He was already there.'

'Any idea what they were discussing?'

Mitch counted out his change.

'Alex wanted to hear Jamie's prison stories.'

'That's all there was?'

'That's all there was. You want that Coke now?'

I nodded. He was smooth. He was plausible. I didn't believe a single word he'd said.

We walked along the road sipping from the can. We passed Poundland. Pound Stretcher was right next door.

'How long have we been mates, Mitch?'

'All our lives. Why?'

'I'm going to ask you a straight question. I want a straight answer.'

There was the suspicion of a sigh.

'Is this about Alex again?'

'I want to know if Jamie is dragging him back into the Tribe.'

'You must know something I don't,' Mitch said.

'Don't play me for a fool, Mitch. Jamie's back. It's starting again, isn't it?'

Mitch crumpled the can and lobbed it into the road. A pensioner protested. Mitch flicked a V-sign.

'Knock it off,' I told him. 'That was an old lady. Don't you have any respect?'

He snorted. 'When did you get your wings, Angel Boy?'

I walked off. 'I'll see you in school, Mitch. I'm going to ask Alex myself.'

'You do that, Ethan.'

At the end of that week I asked for a run out at the Academy. The physio seemed to be taking some of the stiffness out of my knee joint. I had to put it to the test some time. Mum hovered round me while I got my stuff ready. The last thing I needed was Mum being over-protective. I laced my trainers, zipped my bag and shrugged into my jacket. I did my best to disguise my nerves. I couldn't shake the feeling that she had something to say to me.

'What?'

'Are you sure this is such a good idea?'

'My knee hasn't played up for a while. I've got to give it a go.'

'I know.' Her face threatened to crumple into tears. 'Good luck. You're my boy whatever happens. I love you, Ethan.'

'Love you too, Mum.'

I left the house and walked to the bus stop. The only estate agents had closed down. The windows were blanked out with window cleaner. Everything seemed to be closing down: the shops, the pubs, the youth clubs, the Sure Start centre.

Every time a shop shut on the Parade it made the street resemble more closely a mouth with half the teeth missing. The boarded-up windows stared out like brown cataracts. Steel grilles sprouted everywhere.

The Green was dying, but people seemed resigned to staying and dying with it. Everywhere they had to meet or talk was closing, pushing the adults into the living room in front of the TV and the kids out on the street looking for something to do. I was waiting for my bus when my phone buzzed.

'What's up, Mitch?'

'Did you hear about Carl Nash?'

'No, what did he do?'

'He didn't do anything. He died.'

'Say that again.'

'Somebody did him. He took a bullet.'

I felt cold.

'When?'

'Yesterday afternoon. Somebody popped him outside the probation office. A passer-by found him bleeding to death on the pavement.'

I knew the spot. I imagined Carl crawling through the slick of his own blood. The killer had chosen the place of execution well. There was a fish and chip bar that would be closed at that time. The only other buildings were a sheltered accommodation block and a shuttered pub.

You couldn't design a better blind spot to carry out an assassination.

'There's going to be a war.'

'The word is Darren's out for revenge. He says somebody's going to pay for his brother.'

I stared into space then I heard Mitch talking. It took a moment to take in what he was saying.

'See you later?'

'Yes, I'll give you a call when I get back.'

I'd lost a lot of sharpness since the injury. I picked up the ball in midfield. I had to drop deep to get some service. I shifted the ball to my left and went on a run. I'd lost a yard of pace since the accident, but at least I was playing again.

I shoved the ball forward and set off down the wing. The defender kept pace with me and put it into touch. Back when I was playing regularly I would have taken him on. I knew Eddie was watching. I could feel his practised eyes on me. I could feel the critical stare judging my every move. Two years earlier I would have skinned my opponent and managed a shot on goal. I forced myself not to look towards the touchline.

Five minutes later the ball squirted out of a midfield tussle. The old instincts were there. I pounced on it and twisted left then right. The strength went out of my stride. Right away I knew something was wrong, but I drove forward. A tackle came in. I hurdled it and chased the ball. The keeper was coming out to challenge me. I tried to go left, but my leg shuddered and gave way under me. A needle of pain shot through my knee and I crumpled to the ground. As I writhed on the turf, clawing at my knee, the sky raced overhead. Silhouetted faces loomed against the sunlight.

'You all right, Ethan?'

The pain was ebbing. I gasped an answer.

'Yes.' Then steadier. 'Yes, I'm fine.'

I struggled to my feet. I was able to stand unaided, but I could still feel the pain in the joint. I put my foot down, but it wouldn't take my weight.

'Something wrong?'

Every time I tried to take a step my knee buckled.

'I've done something to my leg. I'll have to come off.'

Eddie was by my side.

'Lean on me, son.'

I hobbled off and sat down, rubbing my knee, struggling to hide the hopelessness I felt inside. Within minutes I could walk, but I knew that was it. Dream over. I'd given it a go, but the comeback plan ended here. My old mobility had gone. My knee was never going to be strong enough to play competitive football.

'That's it then, Eddie. It's knackered. '

Eddie was sympathetic.

'It was a knee injury that ended my career. I know what you're going through.'

I nodded. He meant well, but there were no words to express the way I was feeling.

'I'll run you home.'

He must have seen something in my face.

'Don't worry, I'm not going to crash.'

'How is the ticker?'

'I'm fine, especially since I lost a bit of weight. Eileen's got me on salads. A man can only take so much lettuce. I'll be looking like a bloody rabbit.'

I followed him to the car. I stumbled once.

'You OK?'

'Yes, I'm fine.'

I was anything but.

On the way back Eddie kept telling me I was going to be all right. It wasn't what I wanted to hear. The more he said it the less it meant. I spotted Mitch walking along the Parade. I needed an excuse to get out and I'd found one.

'Drop me here, Ed.'

Eddie let me out.

'This is getting to be a routine,' he said.

'Mitch is my mate.'

I nodded and waved goodbye. Eddie looked Mitch up and down then drove off. Mitch had noticed the look.

'Doesn't like me much, does he?'

'Eddie looks out for me.'

'So what am I, trouble?'

I didn't answer. The way he was acting recently, that's exactly what he was.

'How'd it go?' Mitch asked.

My face revealed everything that needed to be said.

'That bad?'

'I broke down. I don't suppose I ever thought I was really going to revive my career.' I flicked a gaze skyward. 'That seals it.'

'Bummer.'

'You're right there.'

'So what are we going to do?'

'Before we do anything, I've got to drop my kit off at home.'

We were almost home when I heard the roar of a

powerful engine behind us. I spun round and saw the Rav 4. The light was fading. Headlights dazzled me. I shielded my eyes, trying to see the driver. Then a shout crackled through the night.

'I want a word with you, Ethan Holt.'

The voice belonged to Darren Nash. The car door opened. I saw a figure scrambling out of the passenger seat. The back doors were swinging open.

'What do you want?'

I was already backing away, looking for an escape route.

'Where's your brother? Where's Alex?'

'What's it to you?'

'Carl's dead. Your brother knows something. Where is he? You can talk to us or we can beat it out of you. Your choice.'

I knew when to run. Slinging my sports bag over my shoulder, I took off. My leg was still throbbing. Doors slammed behind me. Rubber-soled trainers slapped on the pavement. Simultaneously, the car engine snarled. Headlights swept to the left. The Rav was going round the block to cut me off.

'Split up,' Mitch yelled. 'Give them something to think about.'

I was labouring. Pain was throbbing around my kneecap. I knew the identity of my pursuers. My mind was racing. The state my leg was in, I wasn't going to outrun those goons from the North Side Crew.

There was an alley halfway down the Parade, a crumbling wall, escape across waste ground. I cursed Mitch for clearing off. I couldn't believe he'd bailed. I was aware of somebody gaining behind me. I felt fingertips claw at my back. I had a split second to think. I pulled my elbow back and crashed it into his chest. There was a grunt and the sound of him slamming into a wall.

One down.

I'd had to break my stride to take the first man out. My leg gave again the way it had during the match, but this time I managed to stay on my feet. The second chaser was closing. I swung the sports bag off my shoulder and let him have it. He stumbled to a halt holding his jaw.

Two down.

I reached the top of the alley as the Rav squealed round the corner. A door opened and there was a third man chasing me. The other two were already resuming the chase. One was cursing as he struggled to staunch his nosebleed. Blood was spilling through his fingers. I had done him some serious damage. It gave me a grim sense of satisfaction. It also made it doubly important that I got away. My heart was hammering as I hobbled down the alley. Given the state of my leg, the odds were against me.

Then my heart sank. Somebody had appeared at the other end of the alley, cloaked in shadow. Where the hell had he come from? I had one chance. Climb the wall, lose them in the darkness on the waste ground then maybe I was home free. First I had to deal with the new guy. I clenched my fist ... then opened it again.

'Mitch!'

'Get your head down!'

I ducked and felt the rush of air as Mitch hit the nearest man with something hard and heavy. It whipped him off his feet.

'What the hell did you hit him with?'

Laughter.

'Half a fence.'

He was armed with a greasy plank. He sounded almost hysterical. Mad as a rat.

'Where did you come from?' I asked. 'I thought—'

'What, that I'd cleared off on you? Give me a break.'

'Don't know. Maybe.'

'Ain't going to happen, mate.'

I regretted questioning his loyalty.

'I worked my way round the back,' he explained, dropping the plank.

I gave the guy on the ground a quick glance. Blood was spouting from his nose and a gash that ran from his left eye to his ear. He tried to get to his feet. I stopped him with a kick in the ribs. Moans mixed with curses. Mitch was first up the wall. He saw me struggling and hauled me over just as the second man made a grab for my ankle. We fell to the ground on the other side. Mitch was off again, roaring with laughter.

'How close was that?'

I gave him a playful slap on the head. We were both on a high.

'We're not out of it yet. Move!'

We lost the hunting pack on the waste ground. For a while we were blundering about in rubble and bits of tangled metal. Mitch cursed as he stumbled.

'This way,' he said. He guided me past the rusting iron shards that littered the ground.

'Have you got night vision?' I asked.

We hit the road and ran straight into Simmo. My heart slammed. He'd thrown his lot in with the NSC. What was he going to do? As it turned out, he checked the street then hissed an order.

'That way.'

I saw the hollow eyes and something made me trust them.

'Thanks.'

He shrugged and walked away. He hadn't forgotten the night I spoke up for him. We finally made it back onto a deserted road and looked for somewhere to hide until the NSC boys gave up and went on their way. Ten minutes later we were on top of the eighteen-step bridge, one of our childhood haunts. After a while, I saw the Rav on the road below.

'There goes Darren,' Mitch said. 'He wants his brother's killer. Neither you nor Alex are going to be safe so long as he thinks you know something.' He watched the car hang a left. 'What do you make of Simmo back there? Why did he let us go?'

I reminded Mitch of the time I spoke up for him. 'He must think he owes me.'

'One good turn, eh?'

'Yes, one good turn.' I fell back against the wall. 'They nearly had me back there. Where the hell did you appear from?'

'I made an educated guess which way you would go. I saw you coming with Nash's goons on your tail.' He laughed. 'So I went looking for a weapon … and waited.'

'You did good,' I panted.

We bumped fists.

'Man, you did really good. I owe you.'

Alex got in just after one. I waited up. I met him with a question the moment he walked through the door.

'What did you do?'

Alex stared.

'You nearly gave me a heart attack. Why are you sitting in the dark?'

'I didn't want Mum coming down to see what I was doing up. I need an answer.'

'What are you talking about?'

'Darren Nash came after me tonight. Why would he do that?'

Alex managed a shrug.

'What did he say?'

I kept my voice down so I didn't wake Mum. Alex wasn't making it easy for me.

'I didn't give him the chance to say anything. I got out of there.'

Alex relaxed. 'They didn't hurt you?'

'No. He wanted you, Alex. When he couldn't find you, I was second choice. Is there anything you want to tell me?'

He shook his head. He was halfway upstairs when he stopped. 'You did all right, Ethan. I called you a coward. I take it back.'

I sat there with the light off for twenty minutes, maybe as long as half an hour. I rubbed my knee and thought of what might have been but for the accident. Once there had been a way out of the Green, a chance to do something with my life. Now things seemed to be closing in. My mind was racing. Alex had to have something to do with the death of Carl Nash.

There was no moon. The darkness was complete.

10

I find myself wondering when the jaws of destiny started to close. It must have been the discovery of the tickets. It was summer. My exams were nearly over. The tickets were next to the computer where Alex had printed them off. They'd been torn in half. I picked them up and frowned.

'Mum, is Alex in?'

'He said something about going to the Beehive. What do you want him for?'

They were his e-tickets for the holiday with Lindsay. Why would he rip them up like that?

'Oh, nothing.'

I texted him. Why did he rip up the tickets? I tried him twice, but he didn't get back to me. A week later I got my answer. I was at the kitchen table pouring cereal into a bowl. I heard Mum yelling.

'Alex. Alex!'

Mum's voice ripped through the house like a buzz saw.

'Get out here, Alex.'

She kept screaming his name. It was a cry of panic, so plaintive it hurt to hear it. I took the stairs two at a time.

Alex's bedroom door was open and Mum was trembling, physically trembling. 'Get out of bed. Get up right now!'

She had something in her hand, a crumpled sheet of paper. Alex stumbled onto the landing in his boxers, rubbing his eyes. 'What time is it?'

By then I had a fat ball of apprehension sticking in my throat.

'Time you got out of your stinking pit.' She was the far side of angry. 'You're going to own up what you've done.'

Mum waved the sheet under his nose.

'What in God's name do you call this?' she demanded.

Alex saw what she had in her hand. So did I. It was a charge sheet.

'Did you go through my stuff?'

'Don't you dare try to shift the blame. I emptied your trouser pockets so I could wash them. I found this.'

'It's nothing.'

'It's a charge sheet! You're in trouble with the police. What the hell is Section 18?'

It was wounding with intent. On the Green GBH was pathetically commonplace. For a lot of lads kicking somebody's head in was a rite of passage. If your job, your sport, your wheels, your music doesn't make you the big man, your fists just might. On Saturday night our local A & E was a war zone as groups of lads high on booze or drugs tried to get at each other. The only question was whether you were caught. Alex mumbled an explanation under his breath.

'Wounding!' Mum shrieked. 'Did you say wounding?

I knew you were lying the about the attack on Simmo.'
Her fingers were tearing at her hair. 'How bad is it?'

'Mum …'

'Tell me!'

'It's not about Simmo. It's more recent. I got into a fight. I told you. It's nothing. I'll sort it.'

'How will you sort it? You can't sort yourself.'

'I just will, OK? I'm going back to bed.'

She wasn't letting go that easily.

'Oh no, you don't. This time you're not going to stick your head under the duvet and hope the problem goes away. You're going to talk to me.'

Alex folded his arms.

'Fine, what do you want to know?'

'Let's start with the basics.'

He frowned.

She spelled it out for him. 'This fight. Who was it with?'

There was a moment's hesitation.

'Jamie.'

Mum's face was white.

'You fought with *Jamie Leather*?'

She went from frustration to despair.

'Are you insane? You promised me, Alex. You told me there was no going back to your old ways.'

Wounded, he shouted back. 'I didn't plan it, you know. I'm human. I snapped.'

'You hid it from me.'

'I did it to avoid this sort of grief.'

'Thought it would go away, did you? Stick it in your back pocket and forget about it. If you can't see it, it doesn't exist. You're like a naughty little boy, Alex.'

She rubbed tears of hurt and frustration from her eyes.

'That's right, you're like a bloody five-year-old. Only you're nineteen.' She didn't give him time to answer back. 'When did it happen?'

'Last week.'

'Last week! This has been in your pocket for a week? How serious is it?'

He shifted his feet. More evasion. 'Just chill. I'll deal with it.'

She screamed in his face. 'Don't tell me to bloody well chill!' Her voice broke. 'For once in your life talk like a normal human being, not one of those gutter rats you hang around with. Tell me the truth.'

His words came out in a monotone. 'I looked it up on the internet ... eighteen months.'

'Eighteen months!'

'That's the max. It won't happen.'

Then he paused. Mum was on it like a flash.

'There's something you're not telling me, isn't there? Out with it.'

'OK, by the letter of the law, if you plead not guilty and the court convicts you anyway, you can get three to five.'

Mum reeled. 'Three to five years?'

'Something like that.' He had his arms folded over his chest. He was scratching his shoulders self-consciously. 'I just told you, Mum. It won't happen. The jails are full. I'll get community service.'

'You don't know that.'

For a few moments nobody spoke. Mum broke the silence. 'You've thrown away everything, you fool.'

'I told you, the prisons are chocker. They're not going to lock me up for something like this.'

'Get dressed,' she said. 'Put some clothes on. We've got to talk about this.'

'I thought we just did.'

Alex took his time to get dressed. He finally joined us at the breakfast table. He ran his fingers over his scalp, digging his nails into the skin. 'What do you want to know?'

'The fight, Alex: what was it over?'

'Lindsay.'

'This was over a girl?'

'She was cheating on me … with Jamie.'

'Oh Alex! Didn't I warn you about her?'

I remembered the torn-up tickets. He must have done it when he found out.

'I wasn't thinking. I found out from Facebook. Somebody posted a photo of them at a party. They were all over each other. I went to the Beehive to challenge them over it.'

'I want the rest of the story,' Mum demanded. 'Don't hold anything back. I'll know if you're lying.'

'Jamie just laughed in my face. He was taunting me. There was a bottle.'

'You glassed him!'

'No, you don't understand. He had the bottle. *He* went for me.'

'So why are you being charged with an assault?'

He dropped his eyes. 'There's something I haven't told you.'

I saw Mum's face. She couldn't take much more.

'I grabbed his wrist. We wrestled for control. The bottle smashed on the wall. It was the glass. It flew. It went all over me, but the biggest piece caught Lindsay on the lip. There was … OK, there was blood everywhere. The bar staff had to phone for an ambulance.'

There was a moment of shocked silence. Then:

'Oh, Alex!'

'It was a deep cut,' he continued, his voice flat and lifeless. 'She had to have stitches.'

'And Lindsay is blaming you? She's pressing charges?'

'Yes. Somehow, Jamie convinced her it was my fault.' He finished his story. 'The police came round.'

'When was this?'

'You were at work. Ethan was at school. They took me down the station. They found a couple of little splinters of glass in my jacket.'

Nobody said anything for a while. There was no need to put it into words. Alex was in trouble, trouble with a capital kick in the guts.

Mum rubbed her forehead. 'You need a good barrister.'

He needed a miracle.

Alex stared at the ceiling. 'They gave me a solicitor when I was down there. I think it's all in hand.'

I caught Mum's eye. This was getting worse by the minute. I saw the time.

'Look, I've got to make a move.'

Mum sighed. 'I'm going to phone this solicitor and find out what's happening. What a mess.'

'Maybe it's not that bad.'

'Really?' her eyes flashed with irritation. 'Let's hear it then. We've had the cloud. Where's the silver lining?'

'There's Sean,' he said. 'He'll speak up for me.'

'Sean was there?'

'Yes.' He remembered something. 'It's not all bad. There was this other guy too. He saw everything.'

Her eyes flashed as she seized on a scrap of hope.

'What other guy?'

'He came in just before the fight began. He was tall, thin. He had a tattoo on his neck. It was unusual, Chinese or something. He must have seen everything.'

'Did you tell the police about him?'

'Yes. They'll find him, won't they?'

For the next few minutes nobody said a word.

11

The interrogation rumbled on. Mum asked the same questions over and over. Alex's answers became shorter and less truthful. I glanced at my watch.

'Oh, crap!'

After everything that had happened I was running late and it was an important exam.

'Look, I've got to go.'

'Your exam!' Mum said. 'With all this going on, it went clean out of my mind. Good luck, son.'

I smiled a thin smile. Break a leg would have been in bad taste. I turned the corner onto the Parade and saw my bus at the stop. I started to run the best way my leg would allow, then there they were.

'Well, if it isn't Alex's brother.'

I was facing three junior soldiers. So the Tribe's history, is it Mitch? Looked alive and kicking to me. They were in the regular uniform of black trackie bottoms and jackets, Adidas, Lowe Alpine, North Face, Berghaus. 'Tell your brother he made the worst decision of his life when he mixed it with Jamie. He's going down.'

I couldn't miss my bus. Football wasn't going to get me off the estate. The exam mattered.

'Look lads, I don't want trouble.'

'Tough. You got trouble when your brother broke discipline.'

I tried to shove past. One of them made a grab for me. I ducked out of his reach and stumbled away. Mocking laughter followed me. I chased after the bus and pounded on the door. The driver slowed and let me on. I slid in next to an old guy. His face was sad with memories. I thought about Alex. What if the bonehead was right? What if he was going down?

I got to the hall just as everybody was filing in to sit the exam. Some were already sitting at their desks. I found myself following Abi Moran into the room. I was close enough to breathe in her perfume. It smelled good.

'Cutting it fine, aren't you, Ethan?'

'Domestic crisis,' I told her. 'You know the way it is.'

Abi's sympathetic look said she didn't really know how it was. She walked to her place. I liked the way she tossed her coppery hair. The drone of the invigilator pushed Alex out of my mind. There was the rustle of paper as we started to read through the questions. I permitted myself a smile. My teacher had called most of the questions right. The final one was a bit of a surprise, but it didn't give me any problems.

There was the usual post mortem as we spilled into the reception area afterwards. Somehow I found myself drifting towards Abi. She was going through the questions with her friends, comparing notes. There were a few high fives and some screaming. I waited patiently. I didn't scream.

Abi registered my presence and turned to look at me. 'So what did you make of the exam paper?'

'There were no real surprises, were there?'

'No, I thought it was OK.'

We were awkward with each other, but it was a jittery, flirty awkwardness, the kind that means both parties are interested.

'Next stop Sixth Form?'

'Yes, touch wood.'

I took a chance and touched her temple. She didn't seem to mind.

'Are you going to go to uni?' she asked.

'Maybe.'

She cocked her head in a way I liked so I improved on my answer.

'Yes, yes I am. You?'

She laughed.

'Of course. I'm brilliant.'

'Yes, me too.'

Suddenly we were both laughing. One of her friends leaned in to Abi and whispered something. Abi blushed and gave her a nudge.

'What did she say?'

'Not telling.'

The friend was. 'I said you should get a room.'

There were shrieks of laughter. I saw the way Abi dropped her eyes, embarrassed. I decided I liked her more than I'd realised.

'You look good when you blush.'

Abi put her hands to her cheeks. She had freckles.

'No, I don't. I look red.'

I said she was funny, but in a good way. I was trying to think of something else to say when I saw the poster on the wall behind Abi. It advertised a charity night concert. She was one of the featured performers.

'Hey, that's you up there.'

Abi gave me a hard stare.

'Have you only just noticed our posters?' she demanded. 'They're all over school. Do you walk around with a bag over your head?'

'It says you're one of the performers. What do you do?'

'I train seals to play Mozart.'

'No way!'

'No idiot, I sing.'

'Really?'

'Why's that surprising? I sing in school.'

Ouch. I should have known that, but until that moment I hadn't given Abi Moran a moment's thought. It seemed a good opportunity to make my excuses and leave.

'I'll see you around.'

'Yes, see you.'

I was smiling as I left, but there was a surprise waiting at the school gates. A reception party. It was the three boys from the Parade. This time Jason Leather was with them. They were all on mountain bikes. I felt heat steal along my spine.

'What do you want, J?'

I sounded braver than I felt.

Jason grinned. 'What makes you think we want anything? Just being neighbourly.'

He lived over the back. So did the odd rat. It didn't make him a neighbour.

'If you've got something to say, spit it out. I'm in a hurry.'

The superior grin drained from Jason's face.

'I've got a message for Alex.'

'I'm not your servant. Tell him yourself.'

'He'll want to hear this.'

'Fine. What's the message?'

'Jamie says it would be a bad idea for Alex to plead not guilty. Tell him, yeah?'

'I'll think about it.'

'Yes, you do that.' He tapped his head. 'You give it some thought.'

Jason pushed off and led the way down the hill. The riders skidded to a halt at the bottom. Jason gave his parting shot.

'Alex is either with us or against us. There's no middle way.'

I was still watching them when Abi came up behind me.

'Was that Jason Leather?' she asked.

'Yes.'

'I thought he was excluded.'

'He is.'

'Ethan, you need to find yourself some new friends.'

I pulled a face.

'Jason's no friend of mine.'

I walked home with Abi on my mind. The thought of her put a smile on my face. The smile died the moment I opened the door. Mum was sitting at the kitchen table, face buried in her hands. She'd been crying. Sometimes you wonder why you go home at all.

'What now?'

She turned away.

'It's Alex. There's nothing we can do to help him. He's finally done it. Ethan, he's going to prison.'

I had a knot in my stomach. 'What's happened? Talk to me, Mum.'

She pawed the tears away. 'It just keeps getting worse. It's as if I'm in the middle of a nightmare and I can't wake up.'

I sat down and took her hands.

'Take a deep breath and tell me what's happened.'

She nodded. 'Alex hasn't just got Jamie and Lindsay Clarke testifying against him.'

'Who else?'

'There were two bystanders. They were in the lounge. They saw what was happening across the bar.'

'It's a put-up job,' I snorted. 'Where did these witnesses appear from?'

Mum laughed bitterly. 'The Leathers have probably opened their wallets.'

I asked about Alex.

'So where is he?' There was a loud silence. 'Mum?'

She looked away, shook her head, went into herself.

Finally, she turned to look at me. 'You've got to go after him, Ethan. As if things weren't bad enough, Sean's gone missing. He sent Alex a text. He refuses to give a witness statement.'

Sean was all Alex had. I didn't trust the police to find Tattoo Man.

'The solicitor's been in touch with the same story. Sean didn't see a thing. He was on his way back from the toilet when it happened.'

'Is that what he told the police?'

Mum nodded.

'Some friend he's turned out to be. He and Alex have been mates since they were kids. He's sat in that chair. All the times I've cooked his tea for him. I took them both to football. I took them swimming.'

'I know, Mum. I was there, remember?'

'He's going to do something terrible. I know it.'

I was already on my way out of the door. 'I'll find him.'

It took the best part of an hour. There was no sign of Alex on the Parade. My search took me past St Mark's church then on to the Beehive, the park, the playground, the swimming pool that had closed down when I was ten. There weren't many places he could go. He didn't really have any friends outside of the Tribe.

I walked through the estate. The older neighbours were always shaking their heads and going on about how it had changed. They said it was a skeleton of what it had once been, before the flesh of employment started to melt away decade after decade. I would have liked to see the place then, before it crawled up its own backside and started to rot.

I was outside the bingo hall, wondering where to go next, when I happened to glance up. That's where he'd be, the eighteen-step bridge. I thought twice about climbing the steps to check. The Tribe used to gather on the bridge sometimes. The sun was peeking out from a bank of violet cloud. I shielded my eyes and tried to identify the silhouetted figure leaning over the parapet. Finally, I scrambled up the concrete steps. Alex knew I was there, but he didn't look at me. He was watching the traffic.

'Do you remember when we used to come up here as kids? You and Sean dropped water bombs on the cars.'

Alex turned. 'You didn't come here to talk about the old days. What do you want, Ethan?'

'Mum sent me to find you.'

'Well, you've found me.'

'She thought you might do something stupid, you know, go after Sean.'

Alex pulled a face. 'She thought right.'

'Did you find him?'

A shake of the head.

'He's lying low. I would have broken his neck, the yellow scum. How could he do it? How could he sell out his best mate?'

'Fear?' I waited for the word to sink in. 'If you were in his shoes, would you testify against a psycho like Jamie Leather?'

Alex did that thing with his fingernails, clawing tracks across his scalp.

'He's filth.'

'He's human.'

Alex wandered along the cycle trail and dropped onto the grassy bank. He had his arms on his knees. He rested his head on them. I joined him.

'I'm screwed.' He mumbled into his sleeves. 'I am well and truly, totally, one hundred per cent screwed.'

'I thought you said you'd get community service.'

'That was for Mum's benefit. I'm stuffed, Ethan. Jamie's got Lindsay and her slashed lip. He's got Sean and some witnesses who weren't even there. What have I got? Some tattoo guy. The police don't think he even exists.'

'But a good barrister could pull them apart.'

It didn't help. Alex was in no position to get a good brief.

'Yes? What chance have I got, Ethan? I'm just a two-bit scally.'

I suppose I snapped.

'Stop playing the martyr,' I told him.

Alex flipped.

'Thanks for the support.'

I put a hand on his shoulder. 'I'm on your side, but you've got to stop feeling sorry for yourself. We're going to find a way out of this. Maybe there's a witness we don't know about.'

'There isn't.'

'What about the bar staff?'

'Selective blindness. They didn't see anything. Jamie's nobbled them. That or they're just too scared.'

I let the loud rumble of a lorry under the bridge fade before I spoke.

'So tell me about Sean.'

'What about him?'

'You're not going to change his mind by kicking the crap out of him.'

He looked away. 'It might make me feel better.'

'Yes, and it's going to get you arrested again. You've got to start thinking straight.'

After a few moments he gave me his full attention.

'Something's bugging you. You might as well get it off your chest.'

'This isn't just about Lindsay, is it? Something was going on before that. Why does Darren Nash think you know something about what happened to his brother?'

Alex reacted as if he'd grabbed a live cable. 'You're my brother. If you're not on my side, who is?'

'You know I'm on your side,' I told him. 'That's not the point. Talk to me, Alex. Tell me about the shooting.'

Alex started walking. He threw out a hand. The conversation was over.

'Alex ...'

He cut me dead. 'I had nothing to do with it.' He swung round and snarled a reply. 'I've never fired a gun. Never! I only held one once. You were there. It was Bonfire Night, nearly two years ago. It's true, Ethan. I swear on our mother's life.'

12

'Your phone's ringing.'

I came in from the kitchen and leaned across Alex to get it.

'You're going to take root on that couch.'

He didn't go out anymore. He didn't want to be seen on the street. To the Tribe he was a traitor. To the NSC he was a way to get at Jamie. So he made a nest for himself in front of the TV, only moving to get something to eat or go to the toilet. I put the phone to my ear.

'What's up, Mitch?'

'I've got stuff to tell you. You busy?'

'No, I'll come over.'

The street where Mitch lived was more run down than Bevan. Some of the houses had steel grilles and they were heavily tagged by graffiti. Mitch's garden was a rubbish dump. There was an old bedstead and a pile of tiles. A bundle of old clothes spilled from the rip in a burst bin bag. The hedge hadn't been trimmed in months and tall weeds sprouted from cracks in the path. I rang the doorbell and

Mitch answered. He stepped out of the gloom of the hall and glanced left and right. I almost laughed. He waved me inside.

'What's with the cloak and dagger stuff?'

'I'm scared. You should be too.'

The smile slipped from my face. He was serious.

'What's happened?'

'Darren Nash called.'

'Here?'

Mitch ushered me into the living room.

'I had Darren and a couple of his boys sitting right here. I was bricking it. They know I've been hanging with Jamie.'

There were a few bottles of Coors on the floor. There was a full ashtray on the arm of the chair in the corner. I sniffed.

'Has somebody been smoking dope in here?'

Mitch picked up the ashtray.

'Does it bother you?'

'I was just asking.'

He dumped the contents of the ashtray in the bin.

'There. You can't see it. Happy now?'

'Does your mum know?'

He laughed.

'It's her weed. Now forget about the smell. You've got more to worry about than a bit of blow, straight boy.'

I perched on the arm of a chair. It was better than sitting in it.

'So we're talking about the North Side Crew getting out the thumbscrews?'

'Right. Darren's on the warpath.'

'What did he want?'

'What do you think? Alex has been avoiding him and he wants to talk. If Alex won't meet them face to face, you're the alternative route. He isn't going to give up.'

I remembered the chase through the night and the escape over the wall. I ran my hand through my hair.

'Why'd he come to you? He knows where we live.'

'He's not going to go near Bevan Way, is he? Jamie's back on the streets. Carl's dead. There's been a shift in the balance of power. The day the NSC moves onto the Tribe's turf is the day we've got a war on our hands. Nash's crew isn't ready to go head to head with the Tribe. Not yet, anyway.'

Not yet.

'Do you know something?'

He shrugged.

'It's only a question of time. Darren wants a meet with Alex. This is heavy, Ethan. If I don't deliver, they're going to take it out of my hide. I'm scared, mate.'

I felt sick. I had a steel collar tightening round my throat. Mitch shifted forward on the settee.

'So what do I tell him?'

I felt as if I was choking.

'I need time to think.'

Mitch stared at me in a kind of broken disbelief. There were beads of sweat on his face.

'Come on, Ethan. We're in this together, mate.'

'Alex is my brother. I can't just send him into Darren Nash's arms.'

I saw how agitated he was.

'What's the matter with you, Mitch?'

His enlarged pupils gave him away.

'Are you high?'

Instinctively, he glanced at the table. He shoved at a box of tissues, trying to cover something up. He was too late to conceal the wrap of white powder, the drinks straw, the razor blade.

'What, you're doing cocaine now?'

'It's just a little bit for personal use. It's nothing serious.'

'Yes, and what if the police stop you? We're talking about a Class A drug, Mitch. What do you mean, nothing serious?'

'You sound like the teachers. Lighten up. It's not like I'm dealing.'

'Where'd you get it from? No, don't tell me. I'm better not knowing.' I stood up. 'I'm out of here.'

He beat at his forehead with his knuckles.

'I'm getting by any way I can. Have you got a problem with that? This is about the North Side Crew and what they're going to do to me. You've got to talk to Alex. I promised I'd sort it.'

He reminded me of a debt I had never paid.

'I decked one of Darren's crew with a plank of wood for you. What do you think they're going to do to me if I tell them it's no go? The guy I hit, he wants to rip my face off. The moment Darren thinks I'm not going to deliver, he's going to let him off the leash.'

There was only one answer I could give him.

'You expect me to hand Alex over? You can't ask that, Mitch.'

He kept on rocking.

'Don't do this to me, man. Darren didn't ask me to deliver Alex. He *told* me. He went through the consequences if I didn't. By the time they're finished with me, I'll have trouble peeing.'

'I'm sorry, Mitch.'

'For Christ's sake, Ethan. All the years we've known each other! Doesn't that count for anything?'

I couldn't look him in the eye.

'They're going to hurt me. They're going to hurt me really bad. They won't hurt Alex. They promised.'

'And you believed them?'

I walked to the door and I didn't look back.

'You can't let this happen, Ethan.' He was shouting. 'You walk out on me and I'll never forgive you.'

My flesh was crawling with shame, but what could I do? Mum was falling apart knowing Alex faced jail. What would she be like if the NSC got hold of him?

Mitch was still pleading when I slammed the door behind me.

I was at the kids' playground opposite St Mark's church before I paid any attention to my surroundings. I dropped onto a bench and watched the evening sun hanging low over the Green, turning the estate as bleak and empty as its heart. I couldn't help Alex. I couldn't do anything to save Mitch. I wasn't a brother. I wasn't a friend. I was falling into a pit of fire. I sat thinking about football and the accident and what might have been. Was this all I had, a life thinking about a dream that died? Some girls were laughing and shouting as they walked along the main road. Then a voice squirmed free from the general noise.

'Hi, Ethan.'

I knew the voice.

'Abi. What are you doing here?'

'We've been to Emma's. She lives over there.'

She moved out of the sun's glare. She looked good in her school uniform, but she looked even better in jeans and a sleeveless top. She had her hair up. It suited her. I watched a frown form.

'You're upset.'

'I'm OK,' I answered.

'You sure?'

I smiled. 'Yes, I'm sure.'

Her friends were calling.

'No Mitch tonight?'

'I don't want to talk about Mitch.'

'Did you two have a fall out?'

'No. We're not joined at the hip, that's all.'

Her friends called again.

'I've got to go.'

'Oh, right. See you.'

My phone buzzed. Mitch. I didn't answer. When I looked up, Abi was still there.

'Weren't you supposed to go?'

A little of the softness went out of her eyes.

'Is that what you want?'

'I kind of need to be on my own.'

She looked disappointed.

'Hey, don't look at me like that,' I said. 'This isn't about you. I've got things on my mind. Give me your number. I'll call you.'

She wrinkled her nose. 'No, you won't.'

Instinctively, I reached for her hand and felt it warm in mine.

'I mean it. I will.'

She told me her number and I thumbed it into my contacts. I watched her jog after her friends then looked at her number. I added her name to the entry and remembered the touch of her hand. I was going to make that call.

That first phone call was the start of something good. We went out twice that week. On another sunny evening we were back in the playground. This time her friends weren't watching. She sat close enough for her thigh to brush mine. She came closer. I didn't move away.

She pulled out her mobile.

'Do you want to see something funny?'

'You've got the new iPhone. Nice.'

She showed me her favourite talking animal clips. It wasn't long before we were laughing like donkeys and falling all over each other. Her perfume filled my senses and I felt her cheek touch mine. I caught her eye.

'I like your hair up like that.'

She teased me by letting it fall.

'I like it down.'

I stroked her hair and let my fingers caress her cheek.

'Yes, me too.'

We went serious and kissed. There was more laughter then we kissed again.

'Do you want to walk me home?' she asked.

I was getting to like her more by the minute. 'You said you wanted to go to uni. Does that mean you know what you want to do?'

'Yes, I want to teach.'

'Really?' I was incredulous. 'Hasn't going to Broadway put you off? You know what kids are like. What made you choose teaching?'

'You're going to laugh.'

'No, I'm not.'

'Yes, you are. Your voice went all high the moment I said it.'

'I was surprised, that's all.'

'OK, I want to make a difference, work with kids who don't get the best start in life.' She gazed across the estate. 'Somewhere like the Green. Laugh all you like.'

'Who's laughing? You care. That's good.' I waited a beat. 'Crazy, but good.'

'That's right,' she said, still a little defensive. 'I care. So what about you? What's your plan?'

I laughed. 'I don't have one. I just want to go to uni. It's an experience.'

'You must have some idea what you want to do.'

'Not really.'

Abi stopped.

'But what's the point of going if you don't know what you want to do with your life? You'll have all that debt and nothing at the end of it.'

'Life happens now. You pay the debt later.'

She didn't see the logic. Practical, that's Abi.

'Do you know why I want to go? I want something different from *this*. I want to live in a different world.'

'Different how?'

'I don't know. Just different. I'm hoping going to university shows me. Go on, you can laugh at me this time.'

She quoted my words back at me. 'I'm not laughing.'

We crossed the estate talking about things that mattered and things that didn't. We talked about ourselves and our futures. We talked about stuff and nonsense. We talked our way into being an item.

'Does this mean we're going out?'

We reached Abi's house.

'Is that what you want?'

'Yes, you?'

'Why do you think I stopped to talk to you? I've liked you for ages, Ethan.'

'Yes, me too.'

I got away with that one. I barely knew she existed until the day of the exam.

'Really?'

'Really. I'm shy.'

She gave me a long look.

'You're not shy!'

I laughed. 'You're right, I'm not.'

'So why did you take so long to make a move?'

For a moment I was stuck for an answer.

'I was waiting for the right moment.'

Abi seemed satisfied with that. She kissed me goodnight. The kiss was kind of chaste and soft, not like the ones we'd shared at the playground. I had a feeling she had one eye on the living room window. Her parents might be watching. She gave me a hug and jogged down the path to the front door. I watched her inside then I walked home.

If only I'd known that loving me could kill her.

I finally managed to get Alex to go out and do something. He texted me and we met for a game of pool at the Youth Centre. It was the only one on the estate. Even so, there was a leaflet about a protest meeting.

'You mean they're going to close it?' Alex said. 'Isn't anything safe?'

'When did you develop a social conscience?' I knew what was going on in the world. He didn't give it a moment's thought. Sun went up, sun went down. He let things happen. 'Let's play some pool.'

After every shot Alex's gaze roved round the room before settling on the door.

I told him to relax. 'Jamie wouldn't be seen dead in here. Same goes for Darren Nash.'

He nodded. 'I feel better for this break. I was going stir crazy in that house.'

After the game we set off home. We turned left at the bottom of the Parade. I peered through the window of the only café left. The rundown bakery shop was one of the Tribe's haunts. It smelled of fried egg sandwiches and neglect. There was an elderly couple at one table and a young mum bottle-feeding a baby at another while her buttered scone went uneaten. There was a notice board where the plumbers and handymen pinned their business cards. Right in the middle there was a poster about the closure of the library and Youth Centre. The Tribe boys were nowhere to be seen.

'All clear,' he said. 'Let's get a move on.'

I took out my mobile as we set off down the street. There were two missed calls from home.

'Mum? Yes, everything's OK. We're on our way.'

Alex scowled. 'She'll put me under curfew next.'

'Do you know how many times I've got up in the night and found her sitting in the kitchen waiting for you to walk in the door? That's love, Alex. It's one of those four-letter words you don't hear on the street.'

Resentment clouded his face. Then his expression changed abruptly.

'We've got company.' Already, he was looking round for an escape route. 'NSC. Two cars.'

The cars screamed to a halt. One was an Audi. I recognised the Rav 4. Half a dozen occupants piled out. They were aged between fifteen and twenty-five.

Alex tried to make a run for it. I set off after him, but my knee slowed me down. This time there was no Mitch to come to the rescue. The Rav 4 overtook us in a matter of seconds and bumped onto the pavement. The Audi stopped behind us to complete the trap. I noticed one lad with a scar just above his eye.

Darren Nash strode forward.

'You've noticed Scarface, have you? Your mate Mitch did that. As I remember, you left a couple of marks on my boys too.'

My gaze twitched round the group and I located my victims. They gave me hard looks back.

'Ethan only did what he had to do,' Alex said. 'Leave him out of this. I'm the one you're after.'

Darren Nash shifted his attention to his main quarry. He was the NSC's leader and spokesman now that Carl was gone, heart ripped open by two bullets that had thudded into his chest one after the other.

'Long time, no see, Alex.'

'What do you want, Daz?'

'We heard you and Jamie had a fight.'

'Did you?'

Darren eyeballed his troops. 'Listen to this guy. He thinks he's funny.'

'I'm not funny. I'm just not saying anything.'

'Then you're going down, lad. Are you ready for life inside? You're a good-looking boy, if you get my drift.'

'I'll take my chances, Daz. This is nothing to do with you.'

Darren leaned against the Rav 4. 'You think? I see it differently. Maybe you've forgotten what happened to our Carl.'

We let him talk.

'You think you can go it alone, Alex?' Darren said. 'Dream on. If you want to get through this you need a crew behind you. Jamie Leather isn't going to let go. If you're not with the Tribe, you're against them. You need us, mate.'

Alex looked through him. 'I don't need anybody.'

At that, Darren lost his air of composure. He grabbed for Alex. Alex shrugged him off, but two of Darren's crew seized his arms. I tried to get in the way, but strong hands pulled me back. With Alex subdued, Darren took his jaw in a vice-like grip. Pain spread through my brother's face.

'Listen to me, Holt,' he snarled, using his free hand to jab the point home. 'You may think you're clever, but you're just dirt on my shoe. This is personal, extremely personal. Let me tell you a little story. You like stories, don't you? Everybody likes stories. I used to have a brother. You might remember him. His name was Carl.'

Alex tried to struggle, but Darren maintained his grip, gouging his fingernails into his skin while his boys held onto him.

'One afternoon he was leaving the Probation Office.'

Carl had form. He had once cut somebody with a double-bladed Stanley knife. That way it was harder to sew the wound.

'Do you know what day it was? It was our mother's birthday.'

He shoved his face in Alex's. He smelled of tobacco.

'My ... mother's ... birthday. Carl's ... mother's ... birthday. Do you understand? She lost her oldest son on her birthday. Imagine that, eh? There's a bouquet of birthday flowers being delivered when the police arrived. Sweet and sour, North End style.' He looked for a reaction. 'How would your mother feel, Alex?'

Alex grunted an almost inaudible reply. 'I don't know.'

'Of course you don't know because only a mother can know. She's got to live with it every second of every hour of her life until the day she dies. She will carry his death around until they put her in the ground alongside him.' He let the idea sink in. 'Do you know she's still got his present unopened on the sideboard? Have you got any idea what that does to you? Any idea at all?'

Alex swallowed. 'No.'

The fingernails continued to cut into his face. 'Carl walked out of the door and set off home. He had her present in a carrier bag. You know what, he was probably happy. The way I see it, he got careless. He didn't notice the car parked halfway down the street. Here's a question for you. Were you in the car, Alex?'

Alex shook his head. 'No. I don't know anything.'

'That's funny,' Darren said, dropping his voice. 'You don't know anything. Nobody knows anything. It's the Eighth Wonder of the World. Somebody gets shot and nobody knows a thing. How does that happen, eh?

'The shooting happened in broad daylight, but there were no witnesses. Nobody saw who was in that car. Nobody saw who was driving. Nobody saw who pulled the trigger. Do you know, there isn't a single person who can even ID the vehicle. What's that then? Collective blindness? Mass bloody hysteria?' He snarled with rage. 'Maybe it's some kind of official secret. Do you get me? It's one of those mysteries of life. Who shot JFK? Who killed Bambi's mother?' He let the words hang. 'Let's get down to business, Alex. I want to know who smoked my brother.'

Alex was scared. 'What are you asking me for? I already told you. I wasn't there.'

'Maybe you were,' Darren said. 'Maybe you weren't. One thing's for sure, this is down to the Tribe.'

'I've had it with all that, Daz. It's over.'

'You're wrong,' Darren told him. 'It isn't over. It won't be over until I have justice for my brother. It won't be over until every last one of the scumbags involved in his murder is in the ground.'

He pulled a cigarette lighter out of his pocket and thumbed the flame to life. He held it mere centimetres from Alex's face. He stroked the flame back and forth.

'I'm not just going to tug at the weed. I want the lot out, roots and all. I want everybody who had anything to do with what happened to our Carl. Somebody's going to burn for this.'

It was no idle boast. I remembered the Walther. On the estate a handgun was just a phone call away. You could get a machine-gun as easy as calling mail order. A Mach 10, a Mach 11 could be had for £400. The flame hovered just below Alex's eye. It was almost close enough to singe his lids.

'Look, Darren,' Alex said, flicking a nervous glance at the lighter, 'you've got the wrong guy. I didn't have anything to do with Carl's death. You heard what happened between me and Jamie.'

Darren examined Alex's face. 'He took your girl. More reason for you to help me bring him down.' He snapped the lighter shut and walked round to the driver's side. 'I need somebody who's been on the inside, somebody who knows how Jamie Leather operates. I think you're that man. We'll talk again.' He climbed into the driver's seat and lowered the window. 'I'm not done with you, Alex.' He snapped his fingers. 'People who cross me get hurt. Show him what I mean.'

It was a moment before I could make sense of what I was witnessing. Two of Darren's goons bundled an object from the boot. It looked like the guy they burned on Bonfire Night. The limp form tumbled onto the pavement. Then I understood.

'Mitch!' I stared in horror. 'What did you do to him?'

Darren ignored the question and started the engine. The vehicles bounced off the kerb and onto the carriageway. They roared away, leaving me to cradle Mitch's head. He was semi-conscious.

Alex called an ambulance.

▪ ▪ ▪ **13** ▪ ▪ ▪

Nobody put Darren Nash in the frame over the beating of Peter Mitchell.

Nobody pointed the finger.

Mitch himself said his attackers came up behind him. He didn't see their faces. He had no idea who it was. Alex gave the police some story about us finding Mitch lying on the street. I wasn't going to contradict him. We didn't see anyone else. There were no witnesses. That's the way it was on the Green. See no evil. Hear no evil. Speak no evil. It was a code of survival. It was a code of fear.

I visited Mitch in hospital. Mrs Mitchell passed me in the corridor.

'How is he?'

Her eyes were splinters of ice.

'Go and see for yourself.' She swept away.

They'd made a mess of him. He had a tube coming out of his hand. His face was swollen and bruised, his skin shiny. His lips were like cracked slugs. His already small eyes seemed shrunken to points in the stiff, discoloured flesh.

'Oh Christ!' It just came out that way. I saw a tortured slab of human flesh. I saw the result of my own decisions. How could I let this happen? 'I'm sorry, Mitch. I'm so sorry.'

The pinpoint eyes blazed.

'Sure you are. I told you what they'd do to me. I told you and you walked away.'

The words came out moist and nasal, as if Mitch was pushing them through a film of saliva. He continued to force out the words in short bursts, wincing between each phrase. That could be me. Dear God, it could easily be me.

'What ... did you think ... they'd do ... play Scrabble?' He breathed through his nostrils. 'I told you, Ethan. I told you ... what they'd do.'

'Mitch, I had no alternative.'

'Everybody's got choices. You could have prevented this. I begged you to help me.'

I kept trying to make excuses and all the while I hated myself.

'You think I could hand Alex over to them? You think I could do that? He's my brother.'

'Yes, and what am I?'

'You're my mate. Alex is my blood.'

'Yes, well I'm not your mate anymore. I despise you, Ethan. I want you to go.'

I'd made my choice, but the consequences were too hard to bear.

'Don't say that, Mitch.'

'I mean it. I hope some day you look down on somebody you care about lying on a hospital bed just like this. I hope it happens, Ethan, because that's exactly what you deserve.'

'Mitch, you've got to try to understand.'

He looked away.

'I'm done trying. You make me sick. I stuck by you, Ethan. What did Alex ever do for you?'

'That's not fair. He's my brother. Don't do this. Talk to me, Mitch.'

But Mitch didn't want to know. His mum was coming back.

'I'd better go. I'll come to see you when you're back home.'

He answered with a snort. It sounded like contempt.

'Don't ... bother.'

Abi was waiting in the coffee bar.

'How is he?' she asked.

I dropped into the chair opposite her. My shoulders slumped. I wanted to crawl into a corner and die.

'He looks as though he's been run over by a tank. They worked him over systematically. They must have kicked and punched every inch of him.'

I described the damage. Abi winced at every detail.

'How can people do that to another human being?' she murmured.

'Happens all the time,' I grunted. 'Well, it does if you live somewhere like the Green.'

She wasn't letting me get away with that.

'I've lived on the Green all my life, Ethan. I know it's got a reputation, but I've never seen violence like this.' She shuddered. 'It's scary. The people who did this could live in the next street.'

She didn't seem to know about Alex. I would have to tell her sometime. But not yet. We had something. I wasn't going to strangle it at birth.

'Doesn't he have any idea who did it?' she asked.

I took a while to answer.

'No, or if he does he isn't letting on.'

'But he's got to tell the police,' Abi said.

'He won't talk. If he gets a name as a grass his life won't be worth living at all.'

'He can't keep quiet,' Abi said. 'It'll just keep happening.'

'It's going to keep happening no matter what Mitch says or does,' I told her. 'It just might not happen to him.'

'Are you saying we should just accept things like this?'

'What else can we do?'

'Go to the police. Do *something*.'

My mind filled with images of headlights strobing through the darkness, running feet, shouts, threats, a Walther pistol stashed in a glove compartment. Listening to Abi, it was hard to believe we lived on the same estate. How could so many worlds rub shoulders yet remain so separate and distinct in such a small space?

'You make it sound easy.'

I heard the resignation in my voice.

'I didn't say it was easy,' Abi said.

I stared out of the window for a while then I reached for her hand.

'Sounds like we're having our first quarrel. Is it OK if we change the subject?'

She let me take her hand. Her smile was soft.

'I didn't mean to get on my high horse. It just makes me angry to think of those animals getting away with it.'

'Yes. Me too. When's this concert of yours?'

'Next Tuesday. Why?'

'I was thinking of coming along. Are there any tickets left?'

Abi beamed.

'I'll get you one. What about your mum and Alex?'

I didn't hold out much hope for Alex. Mum maybe.

'I'll ask.'

I got home about nine o'clock. The summer light was fading. Alex was sitting in the unlit living room. He wanted to know how Mitch was. I gave him the details, flat and unadorned.

'You OK?' Alex asked.

'No, not really.'

I looked around.

'Where's Mum?'

'She's got a new feller. They left about half an hour ago.'

I took juice from the fridge and swigged from the carton.

'What's he like?'

'Black guy. He drives a taxi.'

I wiped my mouth and returned the carton.

'He's got one thing in his favour. He isn't Declan.'

I needed to share. 'Mitch hates my guts.'

'He'll get over it.'

'Not any time soon he won't. I've never seen him so bitter.' I screwed the plastic cap back on and threw the carton in the bin. 'Any news about the court case?'

Alex shook his head.

'They'll drag it out for ever.'

I perched on the arm of the chair.

'Something I don't get,' I said. 'Why's it been so quiet since Carl took a bullet? Everybody's been expecting retaliation. So what's happened? A big fat nothing. Why don't the NSC just take their revenge? They're not usually bothered about innocent people getting caught in the crossfire.'

Alex had his face turned away. 'You're asking the wrong guy.'

'I don't think so. Why else would Darren come after you like that? There's got to be more to it.'

Alex scowled. 'Leave it, Ethan,' he warned. 'Not another word about Jamie or Carl Nash. Got it?'

I seethed inside for a few moments then admitted defeat.

'OK, you win.'

I stared at the TV. It was five minutes before I realised I hadn't taken in a single word. It felt like I only had one good thing in my life.

That was Abi.

I woke in the early hours. I knuckled the sleep from my eyes and glanced at the alarm clock. It was two a.m. I was still wondering what had woken me when I heard somebody moving around downstairs. I wanted to roll over and go back to sleep, but the noise chipped away at me. After some tossing and turning I kicked off the bedclothes and pulled on my boxers and a T-shirt.

I padded downstairs, stifling a yawn. I found Alex in the kitchen. He was on Facebook.

'What are you doing up?'

Alex lolled back in his chair. 'I couldn't sleep. It's happening a lot just lately. I just keep going over and over this court case.' He scrolled through his messages then shoved the keyboard away from him. 'I thought there might be a message from Sean.'

'Is there?'

'What do you think? He hasn't posted anything for ages. Nobody's seen him. Missing from home. Missing from the street. Missing online. That's about as missing as you can get. Him and this tattoo guy must live in some alternative universe together.'

'You've got to put it to the back of your mind, take each day as it comes.'

'Where'd you get that, a fortune cookie?'

He pushed his chair back. The light from the computer screen illuminated his face. 'Have you been reading Mum's magazines again? My brother the agony aunt. What's the next piece of advice, eh? Learn to be comfortable in my own skin? Well, I'm not. I hate myself. Right now, I wish I was anybody but me.'

'I was only trying to help.' I opened the fridge and found a Dominos box. Picking up a slice, I leaned against the fridge and started eating. 'Is Mum back?'

He shook his head. I chewed on the pizza. I liked it cold. I liked the sharpness of the tomato paste, the chewiness, the gluey texture of the congealed Mozzarella. 'You're bricking it over this charge, aren't you?'

'Terrified. I can't do prison, Ethan, just can't. I'm seeing my solicitor in the morning. We've got to talk about Sean and whether we can get him to testify.'

I finished the pizza slice. 'Doesn't sound as if it's worth a meeting. Sean's bailed on you.'

There was a long pause.

'That's not all we're talking about.'

I waited for him to explain.

'I did something stupid.'

I felt a catch in my throat.

'You know I went looking for Sean?'

The earth was pulling away under my feet.

'There's something I didn't tell you. You caught up with me at the eighteen-step bridge. Didn't you wonder where I was before that?' He took a deep breath. 'I called on Lindsay.'

The last mouthful of pizza stuck in my throat. This was hard to believe, even for Alex. 'We're talking about the one person you were meant to avoid. Why would you do that? You got some kind of death wish?'

'Maybe I have. If you've got something like this hanging over you, you don't think straight.'

I pounded the fridge with the back of my head. 'Tell me you haven't made things worse.'

Alex didn't manage an answer. Powerful headlights hit the double-glazed front door and flashed down the hall. A car parked. There were voices, then a key scraped in the lock. Mum appeared in the kitchen doorway. The car pulled away.

'What are you two doing up?' she asked. She saw our faces. 'Oh no. What's happened?'

I looked sideways at Alex. Mum swallowed.

'What now?'

'Alex has got something to tell you.'

She waited.

'I went to see Lindsay.'

Mum's face was a blur of dismay. Her eyes were wide, her mouth moving without forming words. Finally she forced something out, a word to express her feelings.

Of disbelief.

Of despair.

'Why? Why would you do that?'

'I wanted to get her to listen. I tried to smooth things over. I took her some chocolates … and a card.'

'A card!' The silence seemed to last an hour. 'What sort of card? You wouldn't be that stupid.'

He didn't make eye contact. 'I wrote her a note.'

Mum swore. She took a seat at the table and fixed him with a stare. 'A note? What did it say?'

'I don't remember exactly.'

'Then paraphrase, for God's sake.'

'I said I was sorry.'

It was as if the air in the room suddenly became elastic. Invisible hands pulled it to breaking point. Finally, I put despair into words.

'Do you have any idea what you've done? Run those words through your mind, Alex. Just give them a moment to sink in. Now tell me what it sounds like.'

He buried his face in his hands.

'I know, Ethan. I know.'

'It's an admission of guilt, for God's sake. What else did you write?'

'I said it was all my fault.'

There was a second moment of taut, potent silence.

'What the hell were you thinking?' I said.

Alex closed his eyes. 'I wasn't thinking. I was desperate. I just wanted to make amends. I wanted it all to go away. I'll see what the solicitor says.'

I wanted to shove my fist straight down Alex's stupid, whining mouth. One minute he was the big gangster. The next he was a pathetic, little kid begging not to go to jail.

I could imagine exactly what the solicitor was going to say. The wind boomed against the windowpane. Mum filled a glass of water and sipped at it over the sink. She had nothing more to say.

It was Alex who found his voice. 'I'm sorry,' he said.

What had happened to the would-be gunslinger? Mum turned to look at him, a cold, hard fury possessing her. 'What are you sorry for?'

'Everything. I'm just sorry, OK?'

'Do you know what I want, Alex?' she sighed. 'I want you to stop saying sorry. Yes, if there's one thing I want you to do, it's to think before you utter that pointless, bloody word ever again. If you think you're tempted to say it, do anything, bite your own tongue off. Just don't say sorry. To be perfectly honest, I feel sick every time you use it. That's right: it's just a word, an empty, meaningless word.'

She was quivering with indignation. She started rapping on the draining board with the bottom of the glass, emphasising every few words with another loud thud.

'It comes out of your mouth and it is five letters full of hot air. Do you know what normal people do when they're really sorry? They make sure they don't make the same mistake again. They do this little thing called thinking.' She poured the water away and put the glass on the counter next to the sink. 'Why can't we just be ordinary? Other people go to work. Their kids do well at school. They go to university. They don't have a son who goes out causing trouble.' She threw up her arms. 'They're happy, for Christ's sake.'

Alex swept out of the room. Mum went up soon after.

I stood in the living room and stared out at the sodium glare of the street lamps. There was nobody about. The estate looked peaceful in the middle of the night. The darkness seemed to wash away the dirt. The Green was somewhere to live just like anywhere else. People went about their business, were born, fell in love, grew old.

Only some people didn't get to grow old, people like Carl Nash. The gun took his life. Now his brother wanted to know whose hand was on the weapon.

I remembered the look on Darren's face. Everybody called him a hard man, a thug and worse, but that had been real hurt I'd seen. The papers like to call men like him gangsters, mindless thugs, the scum of the earth. They're still people.

Not the people you want to hang around with.

But still people.

Carl Nash was loved. Or maybe he was feared. Either way, there were hundreds of people at his funeral. The street where he was gunned down had been turned into a shrine. Even weeks later new tributes were still appearing. There were flowers. There were messages that breathed defiance. Others were more personal. They were about the man, not the gang member.

Some of the messages were published in the evening paper at the time.

'U made everybody smile, our C. U were the best.'

'Can't believe you're gone. Your smile will never leave me until you're in my life again. Love ya so much.'

'Carl. Warrior. North End legend.'

There was the promise of retribution.

'RIP, Carl. Never forgive. Never forget.'

Suddenly I had Abi on my mind. I was amazed she hadn't heard about Alex. Sooner or later I would have to tell her.

14

I chose Monday night, the day before the concert.

The scene was our bench by the playground. We were watching the sun go down. 'You can dump me if you want. I'll understand.'

Abi's brow furrowed, but the smile didn't leave her face. 'What are you talking about, Ethan?'

'I need to tell you something.'

She was still smiling. 'Ooh, a secret. Goody.'

'It's Alex.'

'The fight with Jamie Leather?' she asked. Her voice was even, measured, as if we were discussing our favourite films, not a brother who might go to prison. 'I wondered when you were going to get round to telling me.'

She saw the surprise on my face and dissolved into laughter.

'You knew?' I said. 'You let me worry myself sick and you knew all along? When did you find out?'

'A couple of days ago.' She wrinkled her nose. 'More like a week, really.'

'You didn't say anything. How come?'

'I'm not going out with Alex. I'm dating you.'

'You mean you're cool with it?'

Abi tilted her head dubiously.

'I wouldn't go that far. Something you need to know: my Mum and Dad would flip if they knew.'

I still didn't know where I stood.

'OK, now I'm confused. Are we good or not?'

'We're good, kind of.'

She saw my look of confusion.

'Do I have to spell it out for you?'

'Please, I'm a bear of little brain.'

She snuggled closer.

'This thing with Alex,' she said, slipping her arm through mine. 'I won't lie; it scares the hell out of me.'

I gave her a squeeze, instinctively offering protection against the dark shadows that were stealing round the fringes of my life.

'Scares me too. He screwed up, but he didn't mean to hurt anyone. Jamie went for him, not the other way round. It was self-defence, only Lindsay doesn't see it like that. She got cut. Alex was the one with bits of glass on his clothes. Either that or she's making excuses for Jamie because she's going out with him.'

I remembered how Alex had stood by while Jamie stamped on the defenceless Simmo. 'He's weak.'

Weak. The word Alex had always used about me. This was a turn up. Maybe both of us were weak in our different ways. I searched Abi's face for some clue about what she was thinking.

'You believe me, don't you?' I listened to the silence. 'Abi? It's important to me.'

She ran her fingertips over my lips.

'I believe you.'

She took my face in her hands. Her mouth was soft against mine. I clung to her and the darkness that stalked the surrounding streets seemed to fall away.

The hall was packed for the concert. It was a fundraiser. There were pull-up stands, announcing the names of the charities that would benefit. Mum came. Alex didn't. That was pretty much as I'd expected. We sat through the acts, the dancers, the singers, a team of gymnasts.

'I didn't expect it to be so big.'

Forty minutes in Mum tapped me on the arm.

'When's Abi on?'

I flicked through the programme.

'Says here she's just before the interval. Must be any time now.'

Then there she was, walking on stage. She looked tiny, dressed all in black, picked out by the spotlight. That's when Abi started to sing. The power of her voice almost threw me back in my seat. It soared, filling the theatre. Mum gave me a look of astonishment, almost wonder.

'She's good.'

'She's amazing.'

She sang two numbers, standards from the sixties. The first was 'Stand by Me', the second 'You'll Never Walk Alone'. She left the stage to loud, heartfelt applause. I caught up with her during the interval, scrambling through the crowd.

'Why didn't you tell me you were that talented?'

'You think I'm talented?'

'I think you're … Wow.'

She laughed.

'Wow's good.'

Her parents came across. We talked self-consciously, slipped into silences. The lights came to my rescue. They dimmed twice.

'The second half's about to start. You enjoying it?'

I imagined what Mitch would say if he saw me here.

'Yes, I'm enjoying myself.'

People filed back into the auditorium. I was seeing another side to people's lives. On Bevan Way people survived, squabbled, fought, thieved, got drunk. Maybe these people weren't so different, but somehow they came together for a cause, donated to charity, cared about people who had less than they did. They weren't satisfied with just getting by. Knowing Abi was opening my eyes.

'Abi,' I said on impulse.

'Yes?'

'I think you're great.'

Maybe I said it too loud. Some of the people around me turned and smiled. I didn't care. I meant it.

It was July. We enjoyed the long, hot summer as we waited for our GCSE results. The streets baked. The air shimmered with a hot, petrol haze along the perimeter road. Kids hammered footballs against walls or ran wild across the waste ground. They were dog days. For a while nothing seemed to happen. Alex's court case was put on the back burner. If anybody even tried to talk to him about it, he would screw his eyes tight and go quiet. He lived in a permanent present, willing the future to stay where it was, somewhere over the horizon.

He built a wall around the next few hours and lived in

that space. All he had ahead of him was a court appearance that could see him go down for three to five years. What was the point of banging on about it? The law takes its own good time. There's no rushing it. So live with it any way you can.

Endure.

An idea took root in Alex's mind. He was innocent and he was going to prove it.

'That's how I'm going to plead,' he would say. 'Innocent.'

He would see Mum's uncertain stare.

'Do you think I did it?'

'I didn't say that.' She let out a breath. 'Sometimes you plead guilty to get a shorter sentence.'

'I'm the victim. Jamie attacked me.'

'It won't sound like that to the jury. Lindsay is testifying against you. There were splinters of glass on your clothes. Maybe you should cut your losses.'

Alex stood his ground.

'Simple question: am I guilty or not guilty?'

'Alex …'

'Guilty or not guilty?'

'Not guilty.'

Alex savoured his victory. He didn't have many to celebrate.

'So I tell them I'm innocent.'

'No matter what happens?'

'Yes, no matter what.'

There was an uneasy truce on the Green. Jamie and Darren were keeping their powder dry, waiting for an opening. The gangs were too evenly balanced for either of them to make a premature move. But it wasn't going to last. On the Green revenge could come hot and quick or cold, slow, deliberate. The only thing you knew, it was sure to come sometime.

For weeks nothing happened, nothing at all.

The war between the Tribe and the NSC rumbled on without ever catching fire. There was a beating a few streets from the Parade and a midnight spray of bullets through the window of one of the main men half a mile away. Nobody was hurt in the shooting. This time. It made the local paper, but it didn't get on the front page. Guns were old news. There were over a hundred firearms incidents in the city that year. They were so common any incident was met with a weary shrug of the shoulders rather than a howl of outrage.

It would take another dead body to make the gangs' battles headline news.

I was up early on results morning. Halfway down the stairs I knew there was somebody in the kitchen. I gave the door a shove and there he was, Mum's new boyfriend. He was eating toast and thumbing through the messages on his Blackberry. He paused to take a look at me.

'I'm John,' he said. 'John McDermott.'

He didn't look any more comfortable about the meeting than I was. He stuck out a hand and I shook it self-consciously, felt the firm grip. There was an uncertain moment as I searched for the right thing to say.

'You stayed over?'

The words were neutral, but the tone was hostile. John pointed in the direction of the living room.

'I slept on the settee in there. Sorry about the mess. I'll roll up the sleeping bag in a minute.'

I turned. I could see a corner of the rumpled sleeping bag.

'You slept on the settee?' I still wasn't convinced. 'What are you, some kind of gentleman or something?'

John didn't blink an eyelid. 'Yes, you got me. I'm a gentleman.' He spoke with an unsettling honesty. 'Old school, that's me. I wouldn't have liked my mum bringing somebody home when I was your age. I was trying to respect your feelings.'

I expected to see his gaze shift away. It didn't.

'Are you for real?'

'I'm for real. Gentleman John, that's me.'

This was new, a guy who didn't just want to get Mum in the sack first chance he got, a guy who cared what we thought.

'Gentleman?' I said. 'Sounds like you're applying for sainthood.' I was warming to him. 'Where did you meet her?'

'She got in my taxi one night. I drive for North City Cabs.'

'Yes, I saw it parked outside.'

'Don't miss much, do you? We got talking. She's got such a warm personality.'

His voice trailed off. How do you talk to a teenage kid about his mum?

'I'd better be going,' he said. 'Can I give you a lift somewhere?'

'If you're going past Broadway High.'

'I'll drop you,' John said. 'My daughter went there. Give me a minute while I say goodbye to Terri.'

175

His tread creaked on the stairs then there was a snatch of conversation.

'OK, let's go.'

In the car we talked about education. John's daughter got four A-levels at Broadway. She was working as a physiotherapist in Birmingham. The guy was full of surprises. He dropped me at the school gates.

'Good luck with your results,' he said.

'Thanks,' I said. 'Yes, and thanks for the lift too.'

Abi was waiting.

'Who was that?' she asked, following the car with her eyes.

'Mum's new boyfriend. He seems all right.'

'You sound surprised.'

'Shocked is more like it. She doesn't have the best taste in men. She picked my dad.'

'Are you sure you're being fair to her?'

'Maybe not.'

'Let's get our results.'

'Nervous?'

'Not really. I've got a good idea how I've done.'

She was right to be optimistic. When we opened our envelopes it was the expected good news. She threw her arms round my neck. I felt her warmth, the press of her body.

'Look at Maths!' she cried, eyes sparkling. 'Look at Science. I got an A-star in both. This is better than I dared hope.'

'I thought you were relaxed about your exams.'

'It was an act,' she confessed. 'I was having kittens.' She indicated the envelope I was holding. 'What about you?'

I tried to keep the smile off my face, but it didn't work. Abi grabbed for my results.

'Let me see.'

The game was up. I smiled as she devoured them.

'Read and weep,' I said, my breath on her cheek. 'Fancy a Mackie's to celebrate?'

The McDonald's was on the retail park, wedged between Superdrug and Carphone Warehouse. It was a twenty-minute walk. About halfway, my phone rang. It was Eddie. I read out my results.

'I always knew you were a bright lad,' he said. 'I'll be round to see you soon. Keep your head up, Ethan.'

'Always do, Ed.'

My good humour evaporated the moment I walked through the door. I glimpsed a familiar figure at the window table. I hadn't seen him in a while.

'What's wrong?' Abi asked.

'Get me a Big Mac, will you?' I said. 'No sauce. There's somebody I need to talk to. See the lad at the third table back? That's Sean Tennant.'

For a moment she struggled to place the name.

'The one who was supposed to be Alex's witness?'

'That's him.'

She got the food, brought it over and slid in next to me. Sean was trying to crawl inside his own skin.

'On your own, Sean?' I asked.

'No,' Sean answered. 'I'm ... with somebody.'

He still couldn't make eye contact.

Then I saw the reason why he was acting so shifty. Lindsay Clarke appeared.

'Oh, I don't believe it!' I leaned in on Sean. 'You and her?'

Sean's eyes warned me off the subject.

'You're on the wrong track, Ethan. You know who she's going with.'

I leaned my head to one side. 'So put me straight about Alex. I'm all ears, Sean. Go on. Surprise me. Who knows, you might even manage the truth somewhere along the line.'

Sean leaned forward. 'Believe me, you don't want to do this.'

'There's going to be a sorting out here,' I said. 'This is about telling the truth. It's about doing the right thing. I want to know why you stabbed Alex in the back.'

Lindsay edged closer then stopped, standing just to my left. She seemed to be waiting for somebody.

Sean shifted in his seat. 'Ethan, let it go.'

'You're going to hear me out,' I told him. 'I know exactly where you were and what you saw. Alex acted in self-defence.' I softened my voice, appealing to his conscience. 'For God's sake, you've known each other since you were kids.'

'That's right,' Sean interrupted. 'We were kids.'

Sean glanced over my shoulder.

'Lindsay can't help you.'

Then a familiar voice broke into the conversation.

'Maybe I can.'

It was Jamie. Sean gave me a look that said: *I warned you.* I felt Abi tense next to me.

'I've got to go,' Sean said.

He slid out of his seat and Jamie took his place. He spread his feet apart and relaxed against the seat. He took a couple of fries from my meal and popped them in his mouth.

'I've got some news for you, Ethan,' he drawled, enjoying my discomfort. 'The court case is set. It's October twenty-ninth. Alex should have got his letter in the morning post.' He glanced at Abi. 'She your squeeze?'

'She's nothing to do with this, Jamie.'

'Don't tell me my business,' Jamie warned, the smile dissolving suddenly, replaced by a look so intense I felt my heart slam. 'I want you to give Alex a message. He shouldn't have written Lindsay that note. He may as well plead guilty and save himself some serious jail time.'

I struggled to hide my feelings. 'OK.'

Jamie laughed. 'That's what I like about you, Ethan. You do what you're told.' He patted my cheek. 'Be a good boy, and pass it on.'

I stared straight ahead. Finally, I managed to show some pride. 'I'll pass your message on. It won't do much good. He'll plead not guilty because that's what he is ... not guilty.'

Jamie planted a hand on the table.

'Prove it,' he said. 'You should advise Alex to change his mind. If he pleads guilty he might just get away with a suspended sentence.'

He glanced in the direction of Sean, who was walking away. He had just joined somebody I knew.

'Mitch is with you!'

'Are you surprised? NSC nearly killed him. We give him protection. That's more than you ever did for him.' He enjoyed my reaction. 'That's right; he told me the full story. He hates your guts. You can see how things are. There's going to be a sorting out. If Alex fights me he'll go to prison for a long time.'

That was the last thing he said. He walked out with

179

Lindsay, arm round her shoulders. Sean and Mitch slipped in behind him as they walked to the car.

Abi let out a breath. 'He scares me.'

I took her hand. 'Me too.'

◼ ◼ ◼ **15** ◼ ◼ ◼

'It's lovely!'

Abi hugged me in front of her parents, which was a first. We usually had to sit at least a ruler's length apart. No funny business! It was as if I had hopped in a time machine and gone back fifty years.

'Here, you can fasten it for me.'

I was all fingers and thumbs as I fiddled with the clasp on the necklace. Abi's mum and dad knew about Alex. They hadn't mentioned it. I decided to leave well alone. 'Happy birthday.'

The autumn days had yet to turn cold. Abi's birthday was held in the garden of the family home. Smoke from the barbecue hung in the air. Music pounded from the kitchen. Burgers and sausages spat and hissed on the grill. People talked, laughed, sometimes sang along with the music. The embarrassing relative jigged about and tried to get people to dance. Abi led me away from the partygoers.

'How did you know what to choose?'

'Mum helped me … a bit.'

Abi examined the necklace.

'I think she helped you a lot. It really is lovely.' She planted a kiss on my cheek. 'So are you.'

I grinned. More compliments. More!

'Nobody ever called me lovely before.'

'Well, you are,' she said.

Abi's cousins were having a kick-about in front of a mini football goal. The ball rolled to me. I did a bit of keepie uppie and lobbed it back to them.

She watched my face.

'You really miss football, don't you?'

This was somewhere I didn't want to go. 'I don't want to talk about it.'

'It's going to hurt. It was your dream.'

I nodded. 'Looks like I'll have to find another dream.' I went for the romantic jugular. 'Maybe I found it in you.'

She laughed. 'Flatterer.'

That wasn't how I intended it. She wasn't supposed to laugh.

'I mean it.'

She nudged me with her elbow.

'Don't pout. It was said in a nice way.'

I found myself glancing in the direction of her parents. I had something to tell her.

'We're going to know about Alex soon. He's in court next week.'

'How's it looking?'

I ran through the list of prosecution witnesses in my mind, then I thought about the no-shows, Sean and the tattoo man.

'Not good.'

Abi tugged at my sleeve and we walked over to the barbecue to get something to eat.

'Don't mention it to Mum and Dad,' she whispered.

I wiped grease from my mouth.

'I wasn't going to.'

The court case fell in half term, October 29th. It overshadowed everything.

As the day of the trial approached Alex withdrew into himself a little more every day. I lived for Abi and my studies and a new life somewhere around the corner. I was doing well at school. I'd been looking at the university prospectuses in the library. There was hope in all those images of smiling students chatting in the shadow of gleaming campus buildings.

The night before the court case was due to be heard I said goodnight to Abi and jogged across the Eastern Perimeter Road. Whenever I ran I imagined myself back on a football pitch. Then I remembered what would happen if I tried to twist right or left and the momentary smile would slip from my face. One of my laces was undone and I knelt to tie it. A shadow fell over me.

'Hello, Ethan.'

I looked up into Darren Nash's face.

'Don't even think about it. You can't outrun us.'

I straightened up. I saw half a dozen NSC boys. Simmo was one of them. They were leaning on the usual vehicles, Darren's familiar Rav 4 and the Audi A3. It was pointless even trying to escape.

'Big day tomorrow,' Darren said. 'I don't give your Alex much chance, do you?'

'What do you want?'

Darren seemed to consider my question.

'It's like this, Ethan. We've got common interests, you and me.'

I fought to keep my face expressionless.

'Like what?'

Darren relaxed, sitting on a concrete bollard. He waved his boys away and they retreated out of earshot, maintaining a watching brief. Satisfied that he could talk privately, he delivered his opinion in a patient, considered drawl.

'I'll tell you what we've got in common. His name is Jamie Leather. Somebody smoked our Carl. The way I see it, Jamie's in the frame. If he didn't pull the trigger himself, he gave the order.'

'So why's he still walking around?' I asked.

'Don't be stupid,' Darren said. 'If I could take him out I would, but there's a thing called the balance of forces. Carl's death tilted things in favour of the Tribe. We lost our leader, our main man.' There was pain in his eyes. 'Jamie's got more soldiers. Simple as. He's packing more firepower. After they did Carl they nearly forced us off the streets altogether. I'm trying to get back in the game. If I do this wrong, I'll wind up lying in a plot in the crem next to Carl. So if there was a loose cannon, somebody who couldn't be directly linked to us ...'

I was looking for an escape route.

'Don't even think about it, Ethan,' Darren said. 'You're going to hear me out.' He cleared his throat. 'Now, what would make your life easier?'

'Winning the Lottery.'

Darren's face hardened.

'Are you trying to be funny?' He kept his gaze on me

until I dropped my eyes. 'Your mate Mitch tried to mess with me. I'm talking about Jamie Leather. You do know he's going to do everything he can to destroy Alex. The way he chose to plead not guilty, that's got to be bad for his health.'

My skin was creeping. Darren said more with a twitch of his facial muscles than he ever did with words.

'What are you saying?'

'I'm saying the court case isn't the end of the matter. It's the beginning. Jamie's got soldiers inside. If Alex pleads not guilty Jamie's going to destroy him.'

I hadn't considered this possibility.

'I want Jamie out of the way,' Darren said. 'You want him gone too. Like I just said, we've got common interests.'

'So what do you want from me?'

Darren snapped his fingers. Simmo walked to the back of the Audi and popped the boot. He came over carrying an object wrapped in a cloth. Darren unwrapped it slowly, his eyes never leaving my face. There was the ghost of a smile. He was expecting a reaction he could relish. He got it.

I saw the gun and looked round in a panic. 'Put it away! Are you insane?'

Darren smiled with his lips. His eyes stayed cold.

'There's nobody watching.' He ran his fingers along the weapon. 'This is the Agram 2000 9 mm machine pistol. Croatian special forces used it. Any fool can kill with this in their hand.'

I remembered Bonfire Night two years earlier. I remembered the Walther pistol and the way my fingers had itched to hold the weapon. I understood the gun's attraction, but I wasn't a kid anymore. I just wanted to get away.

'I'm not your fool.'

'But you can help your brother. We'll make sure you get away.'

'I've asked you once. Get that thing out of my sight.'

'I can get you a different gun.'

'I'm not talking about the choice of weapon,' I hissed. 'If you think I'm going to do this for you, you're out of your mind.'

'I'm perfectly sane,' Darren said. He flipped the canvas back over the gun and Simmo took it away. 'I can show you how to use it. This is the answer to all your problems. It can make Jamie go away.'

'How is a gun going to solve my problems?' I countered. 'You're crazy.'

'Me?' Darren chuckled. 'You're way off. If you think Jamie's going to go easy on Alex, you're the one who's mad. Alex broke the code, Ethan. If Jamie lets one of his soldiers walk away from the Tribe he's finished. You're his only hope.'

I was struggling to control my breathing.

'Maybe you'd like a little sweetener,' Darren said.

My throat was so tight. Now what?

'I can give you Tattoo Man.'

He had my attention.

'You know where to find him?'

Darren gave a slow, deliberate nod.

'I've always known. Let's say he's a good friend of mine.'

'And in exchange you want me to …'

Darren made a gun with his finger.

'We need an independent force to remove Jamie. You want to keep Alex out of jail.' A look came into his face. It chilled me to the bone. It was a long time before I spoke, but there was only ever going to be one answer.

'Find yourself another mug.'

'Fine,' Darren said, walking towards the Rav. 'It's your decision. I'm sure Alex would understand.'

My heart kicked.

'You wouldn't tell him.'

Darren ignored me, but I got a text as I walked away, telling me to think about it. Darren was toying with me. My senses swam. I turned and yelled a question.

'How did you get my number?'

'You'd be surprised what people tell you when they want to save their skin.'

Mitch. He meant Mitch.

'Call me when you change your mind.'

Not if.

When.

He drove off. Stepping in the road, I shouted after him.

'I won't do it,' I cried. 'There's nothing you can do to make me.'

The cars vanished from sight, leaving the ghosts of red flaring brake lights. Then they were gone.

The day of the trial we got into town early. We killed time in a Starbucks just up the road from the Crown Court. The barristers had their chambers in the area. It was a district packed with offices, sandwich shops and coffee bars. Everybody went to work dressed for business, the men in their sharp suits, the women in matching skirts and jackets, legs sheathed in dark tights. They were the Teflon professionals. Recession and joblessness didn't stick to them. Time didn't weigh on their hands. Some in the milling crowds were carrying paper cups swaddled in brown wrappers. Others had iPhones, Androids or Blackberries pressed to their ears. Everybody walked quickly and with purpose. On the Green people had all the time in the world.

Alex watched the people in suits. He had agonised over what to wear for the court appearance. There was a suit still hanging in the wardrobe. Mum thought getting suited and booted was over the top. She said only villains turned up to court in a suit. She grimaced as she described the look: muscles bulging against the fabric, shaven heads incongruous with the formal attire, necks as thick as a reality TV contestant. It was as good as announcing you were a career criminal. No, smart casual would do, she said.

There were four of us in the coffee house. I sat next to Alex on one side of the table. Mum was on the other side with John. He'd taken a couple of hours off work to give moral support. I messed with my phone. I'd phoned Mitch half a dozen times since I saw him with Jamie, texted him over and over again. There was no answer. He was blanking me.

Soon it was time to go. Alex started out of his seat then stopped halfway. He swore under his breath. I turned to see Jamie Leather walking past. He was wearing a charcoal grey suit and a matching tie. He paused just for a moment to peer through the window. He smiled and mouthed a silent promise.

You're going down.

Mum advised caution. 'Stay where you are, Alex. We don't want any trouble.'

We gave it five minutes then we walked to the court. We made our way through security, emptying keys, money, mobiles into little plastic trays and passing through a screening device. Security staff gave us computerised IDs with bar codes. I consulted a screen and led the way to the right floor. Alex had an interview with the barrister. Mum joined them. I waited while John went over and looked out of the window. Together we examined the seventies décor and the people who seemed to leak out of it. A door opened and Alex wandered over followed by Mum. She looked teary.

'What did he say?'

Alex sat down, arms on his knees, eyes downcast. 'The forensics are against me. Without witnesses, I'm stuffed. He advised me to plead guilty in the hope of a shorter sentence.'

'So what are you going to do?'

His mouth tightened. 'Stuff 'em. I did the right thing when I walked away from the Tribe. No, Jamie attacked me. It was self-defence.' There was a snarl in his voice. Of rage. Of misery. But also determination. 'I'm sticking to my story. It's the truth.'

'What about the barrister's advice?'

'What about it? He advises me. That means I get a say, doesn't it? I'm pleading not guilty. If nobody takes a stand, the bad guys always win.' He glanced at me. 'Like they got away with putting Mitch in hospital.'

I thought of Mitch with Jamie and Sean. I glimpsed Mum's face. It was full of dread.

'Don't do something you're going to regret. Principles are all very good …'

Alex interrupted. 'You're wasting your breath, Mum. Jamie thinks I'll bottle it. That's why he's King Rat. Nobody stands up to him. Well, this time somebody's going to.'

'Even if you go to prison?'

He only took a moment to answer.

'Yes, even if.'

I took my place in the public gallery, next to John and Mum. I had never seen the inside of a court before. The room held few surprises, except maybe that it was smaller than I had anticipated. Justice was meant to be imposing, intimidating. Instead it was … ordinary. I glanced at the judge's bench, empty at that moment, then down at the court reporter waiting to record the proceedings on a stenograph.

The barristers gathered in their black gowns. They were friendly and familiar with each other. Weren't they supposed to be on opposite sides? I wondered. They didn't look very adversarial. I scanned the jury last, trying to read their expressions. Young, old, male, female, they looked surly and detached.

Soon the clerk ordered 'court rise' and the judge entered. Most of the evidence was heard before lunchtime. It was a series of nails hammered into Alex's coffin. All that was left was Lindsay's testimony, Alex's and the verdict.

Lindsay turned out to be a poor witness. Her voice shook and she kept looking in the direction of the prosecution barrister and solicitor for support. Under cross-examination she was flustered and stumbled over her words.

'Miss Clarke, did you see the fight start?'

She shook her head. 'I was texting. The first thing I knew there was this blinding pain in my lip. Then I was covered in blood.'

'So you don't know who started the fight?'

She shot a glance across the courtroom.

'Yes I do. It was Alex. He came barging into the pub, shouting the odds.'

'You've just told us you didn't see it start. I am not looking for your opinion. Did you see it with your own eyes? Think carefully before you answer, Miss Clarke.'

Lindsay shook her head. 'No, I didn't see who started it, but he's the one who had glass all over him. I just …'

'Thank you, Miss Clarke.'

I felt Mum's hand. She squeezed. I squeezed back. That was the last time there was any chance things would turn out right. Alex took the stand next. He stood facing the court, head held high just like he said he would. I felt for him. When you hold your head that high you're asking for somebody to come along and hack it off. The prosecution barrister asked him to demonstrate where people had been standing. There was some dispute over Jamie's witnesses in the bar. Alex said it had been empty.

The barrister seized on his statement. 'How much of the public bar can you see from the lounge, Mr Holt?'

'All of it.'

'Really? Would you like to take a look at this plan?'

He placed a sheet of paper in front of Alex. Alex examined it. There were copies for the jury.

'As you can see, Mr Holt, from no point in the lounge can you see the whole of the bar. You may not have seen the two witnesses, but they saw you. They have stated on oath that you launched an unprovoked assault on Mr Leather.'

'That's a lie! He attacked me. The pub was empty except for Jamie, Sean and Lindsay. Ask anybody.'

It was a stupid thing to say. The barrister fielded the comment with undisguised glee. 'Actually, the court has asked several people, four in fact. They all agree that you instigated the assault. Do you have any comment to make?'

Alex looked away and the barrister wandered over to the instructing solicitor to examine his notes. He took his time before putting the next question.

'I would like to ask you about the assault. Where was Mr Leather when you entered?'

'He was playing pool … with Sean.'

'Mr Tennant?'

'Yes.'

The barrister seemed interested. 'Did Mr Leather address you?'

'What?'

'Did he speak?'

'I asked him what he was doing with Lindsay. He started taunting me. He said horrible things.'

'Would you mind sharing some of them with the court?'

Alex looked at the judge. 'Do you want me to say the actual words? He was swearing a lot.'

The judge gave him the nod. Alex repeated some of the stuff Jamie had said. Two members of the jury shook their heads.

'What happened next?'

'We had a fight.'

I watched the condescending smile spread across the barrister's lips.

'Was it that abrupt? You walked into the pub and a fight started?'

'No, there was a bit of verbal, you know, both ways.'

'You gave as good as you got?'

'Yes, kind of. I was angry about him and Lindsay.'

'So you quarrelled? You were driven mad by jealousy?'

'Not *mad*.'

'So were you calm about him cheating with your girlfriend?'

'No, of course I wasn't calm. How would you feel?'

The barrister glanced at the jury.

'What was said?'

Alex didn't speak. The silence seemed to go on for ever.

'Mr Holt?'

Alex finally chose his words carefully. 'Me and Jamie, we had history. We used to hang out together. That's why I was angry about him and Lindsay.'

'Yes? What did you do when you hung out together?'

He knew he was on dangerous ground. 'We were in a sort of gang.'

'A *sort of* gang?'

'OK, we were in a gang. I wanted out, that's all.'

The barrister pressed him about this, but Alex didn't want to add anything. I examined the faces of the members of the jury. They looked hostile.

'Let's move on to the struggle that developed, Mr Holt.'

Alex swallowed hard. His discomfort hadn't gone unnoticed.

'You say Mr Leather attacked you.'

'Yes. He was going for me with the bottle.'

'You were in fear of your life?'

Alex hesitated, wondering where the line of questioning was going. 'Yes, he'd already hit me a few times.'

'You were badly hurt?'

'A cut over my eyebrow, a couple of bruises. Yes, I was hurt.'

'Such was the severity of the assault you had no choice but to defend yourself?'

'Right.'

Along the row Mum and John dropped their heads. I frowned. Why the sudden look of despair? Then I understood. The barrister was cranking up the questioning, manoeuvring Alex into position, preparing to strike the killer blow. They could see what was coming. The barrister's voice changed tone. Theatrical bewilderment replaced the clipped search for information.

'But you didn't attend Accident and Emergency?'

Alex's mouth sagged open. He knew he'd been suckered.

'Mr Holt? Did you go to hospital with your injuries?'

A long pause then: 'No.'

'Why not? You have told us you were the victim of a savage attack. Did you go to see your doctor?'

Alex shook his head.

'You need to say yes or no, Mr Holt.'

'No.'

'You live with your mother and younger brother, I believe.'

'Yes.'

Ethan glanced along the row. Where was he going with this?

'Maybe they were concerned when they saw your injuries?'

Alex gazed forlornly at us.

'Mr Holt?'

'I hid what had happened.'

'Surely they noticed the cut?'

'I cleaned myself up. They didn't see anything.'

'But I thought you were badly hurt.'

Alex bowed his head. That's when we knew for certain that he was going down. The judge's summing up reminded the jury that Lindsay Clarke had not seen the actual fight, but that the other witnesses had stated on oath that Alex had been the instigator. He asked them to consider whether Alex had attacked Jamie without provocation. Was he in fact the one who picked up the bottle first? There was forensic evidence. Splinters of glass were found in Mr Holt's clothing. Was it his intention to disfigure Mr Leather?

Mr Holt had not sought medical help. Miss Clarke had been the other victim. She had been struck by flying glass. He reminded them of Alex's written note on Lindsay's card stating that the bottle hadn't been meant for her. Did that mean it had been meant for Mr Leather? he asked. Was there any other interpretation? They were back in court in less than half an hour. The verdict was a done deal.

'You have been found guilty of a charge of wounding with intent to cause grievous bodily harm,' the judge said. He would ask for reports. 'This is a very serious offence. You can expect a custodial sentence.'

There was some talk of reports and sentencing at a later

date. I didn't hear properly. The judge had to compete with Mum to be heard. She was sobbing her heart out just along the row.

▪▪▪ 16 ▪▪▪

Alex was sentenced on the last Friday in November. I was finding it hard to live with what I'd done. Darren had been ready to deliver Tattoo Man, but the price was too high. John pulled up in his Audi just as I was about to go inside. Mum was with him. They started unloading the shopping bags. She pulled out the early edition of the local rag.

'Have you seen this?'

I helped them with the shopping and closed the door behind me. Mum laid the newspaper on the table without comment. It was open at page eight. There was Alex's face, the blank, fixed stare that would label him a criminal in the eyes of the world. All these photos were the same. The subjects always had an identical fixed expression, a complete absence of individuality. All you got was a stereotype. The thug.

'Are you in for tea?' Mum asked.

'Not tonight,' I told her. 'I'm seeing Abi.'

I got to Abi's house about five o'clock that afternoon

and rang the doorbell. Unusually, Mr Moran came to the door rather than an excited, welcoming Abi. There was a shake in my voice as I asked where she was. I had an idea what was coming.

'Is she in?'

'We saw the newspaper, Ethan.'

I'd tried to prepare myself for this moment. Now that it had come I didn't know what to say.

He cleared his throat. 'I've got to think about Abi's safety.'

I was indignant. 'She's safe with me. I would never let anything happen to her.'

'Ethan, you're not going to get the chance.'

'Just give me five minutes,' I said. 'Please.'

In a gesture of impatience Mr Moran exhaled sharply. He took a step back and started to close the door.

'Listen. I said listen!' I put my foot in the door. 'Jamie Leather's scum. He framed my brother.'

Mr Moran wasn't listening. 'Take your foot out of the door, Ethan and stop shouting.'

'I'm not my brother. I haven't done anything wrong. I'm not involved in gangs. Believe what you like about Alex. I can't do anything to change that. But I can't be held responsible for his actions.'

Nothing I said made any difference.

'I will ask you one more time, Ethan. Remove your foot from the door.'

I admitted defeat and stepped back. The door clicked shut. I stood in the street with my heart kicked out. I took a step back and shouted Abi's name. I leaned against a wall and lowered my head, wishing I could walk back through time and be in the Beehive the night

Alex and Jamie had fought. There was no going back. What was done was done. I would have to live with the consequences. Just like Alex. One bottle, one frightened kid trying to protect himself and the fallout had changed all our lives. I started for home then I heard a shout.

'Ethan!'

It was Abi. She was racing down the hill, hair flying. She threw herself into my arms and covered my face with a carpet of kisses.

'They let you come?'

'I didn't ask their permission. They can't keep me prisoner. Nobody's going to stop me loving you, Ethan.'

I gave a nervous laugh.

'You love me?'

She looked surprised at what she had said then laughed.

'Dead right I do.'

'And you came to tell me that?'

'I wanted to let you know nothing would keep us apart.'

I leaned my forehead against hers.

'You're insane, you know that.'

'Only because you made me this way.'

Tyres hissed on the road. It was Mr Moran coming looking for her.

'I've got to go, Ethan, but don't worry. We're together as long as you want me.'

I watched her and tried to imagine the conversation between father and daughter. Then I turned to go. The sun had just come out.

I couldn't believe it. Abi had stuck up for me. The smile started to fade from my face as I made my way along the

Parade. What right did I have to be happy while Alex was rotting in a cell? I turned the corner and stopped. Blood rushed in my head. It was them.

'Here he is, boys.'

Dean and Jason pushed off the garden wall where they'd been sitting. There were half a dozen gang members with them. Mitch was there, standing at the edge of the group, slightly detached. Yellowed fingers zipped up black jackets. A few of the neighbours had gathered, watching events. Jamie wasn't there.

'What's up, Ethan? Aren't you pleased to see us?'

I tried to get inside. I concentrated on keeping my pace regular and unflustered. I was determined to face them down. I asked a question, deadpanned it. 'Is there a problem, Dean?'

'Problem?' Dean said with a smirk. 'Who said there was a problem?' He examined each of his accomplices in turn. 'Have you got a problem? What about you at the back? See. Nobody's got a problem.'

Some of the neighbours had assembled down the road. The group was made up of older people. They were uncertain what to do. One was tapping her mobile symbolically against her teeth. The gesture said everything. Using it was always going to be a step too far.

'It's OK,' Dean announced. 'We're just having a word with our friend, Ethan.'

'You're no friends of mine.'

I had my fists clenched, but I had never been in a worse position to put up a fight. Dean was enjoying my discomfort.

'Oh, now you're hurting my feelings.'

'I'm telling you to go.'

Dean sat down and folded his arms. All around him the Tribe hooted and clapped. Mitch was the only one who watched in silence. It was up to me to make the next move.

'Fine,' I said, wishing there was a way to wipe the smirk off Dean's face. 'You've made your point. So what is it you want?'

Dean lolled back on the wall and watched a seagull wheel overhead. After a few moments spent watching the bird's movements he said, 'I think we got what we wanted, don't you?'

'Meaning?'

'Meaning your Alex is where he belongs.'

'Fine, you've won. You got him sent down.' I looked at the crowd, searching for a clue. How was I meant to react? My heart was slamming, but I was managing to hide my feelings. At least I hoped so. 'So what are you doing here? You got Alex locked up. It's over.'

Dean squinted up at me. Bullies usually get themselves in a position where they can look down at their victim. Dean's relaxed body language was saying he could take the inferior position and still be in control. The gang was his guarantee. He said something designed to let the demons out.

'That's what Jamie wanted me to tell you. It isn't over.'

It was a while before I spoke.

'What more do you want from us?'

'Jamie wants his boy back.'

'Alex?'

'That's right.' He let it sink in. 'He wants Alex. He wants you too.'

This didn't make any sense.

'Are you trying to be funny?'

'Do I look like I'm wearing a red nose?'

'What if Alex did come back?' I demanded. 'You would never trust him.'

Dean's face had a look of bored amusement. 'It's not about trust. It's about obedience. We give the orders. You take them. Today, tomorrow, for ever. It isn't over because it will never end. You belong to us. It's for keeps.'

I was thunderstruck.

'We've already told you, Ethan. Nobody walks away. Alex was inner circle, a soldier. He doesn't get to quit. It isn't an option.'

'So this is all about saving face?'

'It's about being a brother.'

'And me? Why me?'

'It's like this,' Dean said. 'If we let Alex walk away, people start to see us as losers. We're giving a green light to the competition. But if Alex comes back with his tail between his legs we can call it quits.'

I was still digesting the words when Dean delivered the punchline.

'Only that's not enough either. That would just leave things as they are. It wouldn't be much of a result, would it? We've got to come out winners.'

'Is that what you need me for … some kind of trophy?'

'A trophy, yes, that's it. Nicely put. We'll display you in our cabinet for everybody to see. You'll be living proof that nobody's going to take us on and get away with it. You're with us or you're against us. You come back to us on your knees or we break you. We don't really care which.'

I walked away. 'Forget it, Dean. I'm not playing.'

I heard the scrape of Dean's shoes as he stood up. 'Don't defy us, Ethan. You won't like the consequences.'

I turned. 'What consequences?'

Dean ignored me. With a nod of his head, he dismissed the Tribe. They broke up into twos and threes and dispersed. Jason jogged after Dean as he set off towards the Strand.

I pursued the departing brothers. 'What consequences?'

'We know a few boys inside,' Dean said, tossing away the remark like a sweet wrapper.

Heat washed down my spine. 'What's that supposed to mean?'

'They've got orders.' A shrug accompanied the knowing grin. 'You know, we've told them to help Alex settle in.'

'You don't touch him,' I shouted. 'Hear me? You leave him alone!'

Dean was all superiority and contempt. 'Or what?'

I didn't answer.

They were right.

Or what?

Mitch stayed behind when the others left.

'What are you doing with them? They came to my home, Mitch. You can't think that's right.'

That's when he said his piece.

'Forgotten who you're talking to, Ethan?' His face twisted into a sneer of contempt. 'Where were you when the NSC were putting me in hospital? There's a war going on. Now it's come to your doorstep you're the one squealing. Where were you when I needed you, Ethan? What happened to friendship then?'

'I've said I'm sorry.'

'You think that makes it all right? You're good with words, Ethan. Trouble is, it takes more than words to make things better.'

I heard him out.

'So tell me what it takes.'

Mitch let his gaze drift away across the estate.

'Maybe it takes you to feel the way I felt.' The cold eyes were back. 'Yes, maybe it takes you having to experience the same kind of crap I've had piled on me.' Then he repeated something he'd said in hospital. 'I hope you get to see somebody you care about lying in a hospital bed. When that happens you're going to see me laughing.'

'That's sick, Mitch. What kind of friend are you?'

'Same kind of friend you were to me. One day you are going to hurt the way I did and I'm going to enjoy it.'

With that he was gone, marching away towards the Parade. I thought about calling him back then I dismissed the idea. What was the point? Our friendship was broken for good. But even then, I couldn't imagine the depth of his hatred.

I heard Mum come in.

'Who were you talking to?' I asked.

'Trick or treaters. Good job I remembered to get a few multi-packs of sweets. They egged the window last year.'

She was smartly dressed.

'Where have you been?' I glanced at the smart skirt and blouse. 'You're all dressed up.'

'I had an interview.'

'What for?'

'There was something going on the radio at North City Cabs. I'm fed up of the dry cleaners.'

'This the same North City Cabs where John works?'

'Yes, he put in a word for me. I don't know whether I'll get it. There were half a dozen young girls. One of them had a degree.'

'She went to uni?'

'That's how you usually get a degree.'

'So why does she want to work for a cab firm?'

'There's nothing else. What have you been doing with yourself?'

'I saw Mitch.'

I didn't mention the Tribe.

Mum shrugged off her jacket and hung it up.

'I thought you two had fallen out.'

'I saw him, that's all.'

'Well, steer clear, Ethan. I've heard things.'

I didn't ask what things.

Jamie wasn't done with me. The roar of a car engine tore me out of a fitful sleep. The alarm clock told me it was two in the morning. I swung my legs out of bed and stumbled to the window. Headlights blazed and smeared the rain-pebbled windows with an oily, yellowish glare. Somebody was pounding the horn. I recognised the car.

'Jamie.'

I stood at the window, fear roaring in my head. Then I heard Mum moving about. I squirmed into my tracksuit bottoms and stumbled out on the landing. She was emerging from her room, knotting the belt of her dressing gown.

I waved her back. 'Stay inside.'

'What do they want?'

My heart was hammering. What if they got in? I had to check the locks.

Mum was yelling after me.

'What are you going to do?'

Truth is, I didn't know. Instinct was driving me.

'Stay where you are,' I told her.

I rushed downstairs into the searing beam of the headlights. They strobed through the gloom of the living room. I had just stepped into a nightmare. The smell of fear was on my skin. It was the idea of them invading the house, the thought of being trapped. I shielded my eyes, reached the far wall and twitched at the blinds. It wasn't just the Subaru. There was another vehicle. It was slewed across the road. Rap was blaring from the speakers. The Tribe had their anthem thumping in the night. House lights sprang to life across the road as the noise woke the neighbours.

Half-blinded by the flash of the headlights, I started to make out the silhouetted figures of the driver and front seat passenger.

Finally, I came to a decision. I armed myself. There was a baseball bat in a downstairs cupboard, probably something to do with Declan. I yanked the door open and grabbed the handle. My hands were clammy with fright. Then I waited by the front door. My senses were spinning. Were they going to try to force their way in? The vehicle's driver hit the horn. There was a loud blast. Then two more. That's when I heard their voices.

'Trick or treat, Ethan. Trick or treat.'

That was Jason's mocking tone. I worked out the arrangement in the Subaru. Jamie was driving. Dean was in the passenger seat. There were a couple of others in the back. I wondered if Mitch was one of them. The vehicle reversed at high speed then roared forwards again, the headlights sweeping the living room a second time. Jamie repeated the manoeuvre several times, reversing, braking, roaring forward. Each time Dean and the others repeated the taunt. *Trick or treat.*

I heard footsteps behind me and spun round. 'I thought I told you to stay upstairs.'

'Don't give me orders, Ethan. I'm your mother.'

There was another noise.

'What are they doing?'

It was the turn of the second vehicle. It was a monster. It had bull bars. The driver advanced right up to the garden wall. The vehicle edged forward slowly until the brickwork gave way. The wall wasn't much to start with. Now it was a pile of rubble on the threadbare lawn.

Suddenly fear was transformed into rage. Without thinking, I threw the front door open and ran into the headlights. I stood in the road, eyes darting from one vehicle to the other. I was barefoot. Bare-chested. Mum was screaming for me to come in. I ran at the Subaru, but Jamie reversed down the road and stopped. I sprinted out into the street, beside myself with impotent fury.

'You want me, Jamie? You want me? Why don't you get out of the car?' My voice was hoarse, a mixture of fear and anger.

The Subaru rolled back, teasing, taunting. Trick or treat.

I ran into the road. 'Come on!'

What I was doing was madness. A siren wailed in the distance, mixing with Mum's screams for me to come back. The siren slashed the darkness. One of the neighbours must have phoned the police. I watched the four by four take off and walked back to the house, gasping down gulps of air.

'Why did you do it?' Mum cried through her tears. 'What made you run out like that? You could have got yourself killed.' She beat her fists against my chest then clawed, sobbing, at my face. 'Don't you understand, Ethan? Don't you get it at all? I've got one son in a Young Offenders' Institution. I don't want the other one dead.

I walked past her into the house. I put the bat away.

'I don't want this in my hand when the police come.'

But the police didn't come. The siren was nothing to do with me, nothing to do with the Tribe. It was just a coincidence. A crime had been committed somewhere else on the estate. I was about to go inside when I saw the calling card. It was a pumpkin with the usual macabre face. But whoever had cut its features had left the knife behind.

It was sticking out of the Halloween head.

17

It was cold that November. The Arctic winds howled in, bringing unseasonal snow and ice. The city shuddered. There were more empty buildings on the Parade. The Sure Start centre closed down. Two shops followed. People talked about the state of the place, the boarded up frontages, the litter and debris, but nobody thought they could do anything about it. Nobody expected anything to change. The anger was there, but it didn't catch fire. New graffiti appeared: *is there life before death?* It wasn't original, but it summed up the mood. Rage would take over later.

The Tribe boys were always there, huddled together, stamping and pounding their black gloves. Jamie Leather rarely put in an appearance, but he was in the background, pulling the strings. The gang visited our house three more times over the next week. They always left a calling card. The first time it was a dead rat, the second a rope knotted into a noose. They hung it in front of the door. The third time they spray canned a message on the wall opposite.

The Tribe.

With us or against us.

They understood that it isn't the punch that terrorises the victim, but the threat of the blow. They wanted to drive us to distraction. I sat in the Sixth Form centre, withdrawn, yawning, waiting for Abi to arrive. The instant she saw me there was concern in her face.

'Have they been around again?'

'Alex isn't the only one who's in prison. Mum's scared to go out. John does his best when he's around. He rebuilt the wall. If they turn up when he's there he goes out and has a go.'

'Do they take any notice?'

I gave a weary shake of the head.

'They laugh in the face of the police. A cab driver isn't going to worry them.'

I seemed to be walking on a sheet of glass gazing into the endless darkness below. Every day I had this vice fixed to my skull. Somebody was turning it, twisting it, tighter, tighter, increasing the pressure so I felt as if my head would snap in two. I hated visiting Alex inside. My gaze flitted round the institutional walls, the harsh lighting. The whole place was designed to scream hopelessness. Mum caught my eye and gave me a sympathetic smile. We sat at a table one row from the wall, three from the door. A prison officer stared down the aisle with unfocused eyes, thinking of family, thinking of kids, bored by the scene before him. Finally Alex entered and made his way towards us.

Mum rose to her feet and cried out. A few heads turned.

'Your face, Alex. What happened?'

He dropped into the seat opposite, raising a hand

instinctively to the right side of his face, probing tenderly at the swelling. It was puffy and dark with bruising. 'Officially, I fell in the shower.'

'The truth,' Mum demanded. 'What really happened?'

'Unofficially, the Tribe happened. Jamie knows people in here.'

I imagined bare feet padding on tiled floor, punches to the kidney and ribs, Alex's face jammed into the shower button. Then there was pain and the swirl of blood in the draining water.

'Did you report it?' Mum demanded.

Alex shrugged. 'What's the point?'

She was halfway out of her chair, ready to rip into the warder.

'Leave it, Mum.'

'What?'

'Leave it, OK?'

She stared him out. 'I will not leave it. They can't be allowed to get away with this.'

I twisted my head to see what she was going to do. The warder saw her coming. He did his best to deflect her anger, but she was in no mood to be pacified. Her raised voice attracted some attention from the visitors around the room. One laughed. Others shook their heads. The warder ushered her into a side room.

'Look at her,' I said, nodding towards the window through which she could be seen haranguing the warder. 'She's got guts; you've got to give her that.'

Alex was staring right through me.

'Oh, she's got guts.' he said. 'What about you, Ethan?'

They were the words I had dreaded ever since Darren made his threat. I had a sliver of ice in my heart.

'What do you mean?'

Alex's eyes stayed on me.

'I know, Ethan. I know Darren Nash offered to keep me out of prison. Why didn't you tell me?'

'How did you find out?'

'Does it matter?'

'You don't know what he wanted in exchange.'

'I can imagine.' Alex killed my explanation with a frown.

Then Mum was back, oblivious to the tension between us.

'He says he's going to file a report. My son gets beaten to a pulp and he writes a report! They ought to let me in there. I would go straight up to the cowards who did it and tell them what I think of them.'

I felt so proud of her at that moment. Not Alex. He knew what the consequences could be.

'Tell him you made a mistake,' he said. 'Please Mum. It's only going to make things worse.'

'Are you serious? Forget it, Alex. I'll never stop fighting for you.'

A silence followed. It continued down the corridor and out through the gates.

I went looking for Jamie that night. I walked the streets knowing Alex thought I'd betrayed him, knowing he thought I was weak. Finally the familiar Subaru made an appearance. Jamie got out, flanked by Mitch and his brothers.

'So we've got a deal?' he said. 'You and Alex are my boys.'

I could barely breathe. I tried to keep my voice even.

'There's no deal,' I told him. 'We don't want anything to do with you and your gang.'

Jamie's face clouded. 'So why did you want to see me?'

Scared as I was, I pushed out the things I had to say. 'To put you straight.' For a moment I was on the front foot. I'd managed to take Jamie completely by surprise. 'I'm telling you to lay off my family.'

Jamie stared for a few moments then he burst out laughing. Dean and Jason joined in.

'There's a comedy evening at the Beehive. They're having an Open Mic Night. You should go.' A pause. 'You made us laugh.'

'Just leave us alone, OK?' I said. 'Let Alex do his time. He can't do you any harm. We just want a quiet life.'

'Alex should have thought about that when he pleaded not guilty. That was a challenge to my authority, Ethan.'

'There's got to be a way out of this.'

Jamie thought for a moment and smirked. 'OK, I'll throw you a bone.'

I didn't like it when he smiled.

'Fight our Dean,' Jamie said. 'If you beat him, I'll let it drop.'

'Is this some kind of joke?'

'No joke, Ethan. Call it a straightener.'

I was wary.

'This is legit? It's just me against him?'

'We have a code of honour, Ethan. Isn't that right, Mitch? We don't rat on our mates.'

Any other time I would have laughed in Jamie's face, but I was desperate. I wanted to stop hurting. I wanted to sleep. I started to shrug off my jacket. Dean didn't wait for me to put it to one side. With my arms restricted, he launched a flurry of punches. One rocked me back, tearing the breath out of my chest. The second slammed into the side of my head, numbing one side of my face. I fought my way out of the jacket, still taking blows to my head, chest and shoulders. I half-turned, taking another punch on the back of my head. I stumbled away with my back to Dean, desperate for a few seconds to clear my head. Dean came forward, kicking the back of my knee.

'Had enough, Holt?' Dean demanded.

The taunt gave me a split second to claw my way out of the booming pain that had enveloped me. I snapped my elbow back into Dean's face and heard the grunt of surprise. I spun round and brought my forehead down on his nose. We crashed to the pavement punching and cursing. I was on top.

The exhilaration only lasted a second. The moment I got the upper hand, the world exploded around me. Gloved fingers gouged my eyes. A fist snapped into my ribcage sending waves of pain roaring through me. I was at the centre of a howling storm of savage blows. I flailed frantically, trying to land a punch. The world around me seemed to shatter into fragments, torn images of racing storm clouds, streetlights and silhouetted figures. Then, as quickly as it had started, the ferocious onslaught was over. I heard the thud of fleeing footsteps. I was aware of a flashing blue light.

'Are you all right?'

I squinted at the newcomer, a cop in a stab vest.

'I think so. Yes.'

'Do you know who attacked you?'

I thought of Alex in prison and shook my head.

'Do you want me to call an ambulance?'

'I'm fine.'

'You don't look fine.' He reached for his radio. 'I'll get you some help.'

'I don't want you to. Leave me alone.' Then I lowered my voice. 'Sorry, I know you want to help, but I'm all right, OK?'

'Look,' he said, 'if you know who did this to you, you've got a duty to report it.'

'They took me by surprise. I didn't see their faces.'

Same crap Mitch had given the police and Simmo before him. Nobody talks.

'So you're saying it was an unprovoked assault?'

'I'm saying I want to go home. Thanks for arriving when you did, but I've got nothing to say.'

'We'll give you a lift.'

I was horrified.

'You think I'm going to be seen getting out of a police car? On Bevan? Do you have any idea how that would look?'

The copper exchanged glances with his partner.

'Look,' I said. 'If you want to help, just leave me alone.'

It took me twenty minutes to complete the walk home. It usually took ten. Several times I had to sag back against the hedges on the way and suck in lungfuls of air. My ribs were as sore as hell.

'Oh, Jesus no,' Mum cried the moment she saw me. 'What happened?'

'I got into a fight.'

'Don't tell me. You went looking for Jamie, didn't you? How could you?' She scrambled out of her chair and brushed back my hair, examining the damage. 'Your eye's half-closed.'

I tried to make a joke of it.

'You should see the other guy.'

'Don't you even try to make light of it,' she said. 'What happened?'

'You're right,' I admitted. 'I went after Jamie. I wanted to know what it would take for him to lay off Alex.'

'And this was his answer?'

'He came mob-handed,' I told her. 'Fists and boots were coming at me from every direction.'

Mum did her best to clean me up. I refused to go to A & E. I lay in bed with the pain. I watched headlight beams flashing across the walls and clenched my fists. This would never end, not as long as Jamie was out there.

18

Autumn turned to winter. The last of the dry, fallen leaves skipped down the Parade. They turned to damp mulch then to a frozen, brown smear on the glassy pavements. The Tribe boys were no longer a permanent presence outside the house, but they hadn't gone away. They stood on street corners, breath misting the still, cold air. They toured the streets on their bikes, the inner circle preferring Jamie's Subaru. People watched, knowing who they were, aware of their reputation, nervous about their capacity for retribution. They wondered how they could run their vehicles. They didn't ask.

The Tribe didn't go away. Jamie's reach stretched to prison. Alex was living in fear so Mum went to war for her boy. She talked to anyone who would listen. John gave her what support he could. She pounded on doors, shouted in the face of authority. She even wrote to her MP. A week before Christmas it paid off. The phone rang, urgent and shrill. I picked up.

'Yes?'

There was a silence then Alex's voice.

'It's me.' It was Alex. 'Put Mum on.'

He knew what Darren wanted. I think he understood. Given his situation, it was just about impossible to talk it through. I was on my way back into the living room when she screamed.

I rushed back. 'Mum?'

'It's all right,' she said. 'They're moving Alex. They've finally agreed to give him some protection. I'm so pleased, Alex. Talk soon.'

She was beaming.

'This is down to you, Mum, nobody else.'

'Yes, I did it, didn't I?'

She dropped into her chair then leapt back out of it. She was full of energy.

'I've got another piece of news for you.'

I waited.

'John wants us to get married. He's saved the deposit for a house. We're going to start looking. Ethan, this is our chance. We're going to start over.'

She reached for her bag and stuck twenty pounds in my fist.

I stared at it. 'What's this for?'

'Take Abi out,' she said. 'My treat.'

I wanted to hug her. I hadn't felt comfortable calling on her since Alex went down. Her parents didn't say much. They didn't have to. Abi would come round to mine, but there weren't many places we could be together.

'You sure you can afford it?'

'For my brilliant son? Yes, I can afford it.'

She hadn't been this happy in a long time. On impulse, I kissed her on the cheek and reached for my jacket.

'Ethan,' she said.

'Yes?'

'We're going to be OK.'

Mr Moran let me in. I don't know how she did it, but Abi was starting to win her parents round. I can't say they looked overjoyed to have me back in their house and it still felt like walking on eggshells, but they didn't try to show me the door. I found her at the computer, putting the finishing touches to her assignment. I checked that nobody was watching and planted a kiss on the nape of her neck. She gave a little shiver of appreciation and reached back to squeeze my arm.

'Don't distract me,' she said, half-turning so I could see the way the shadows danced on the planes of her face. 'I'm onto the conclusion. Have you got yours done?'

'Not yet,' I told her, 'but I'm on my way.' I waved the twenty pounds under her nose. 'Fancy the cinema?'

She turned. 'You're in a good mood. What's the occasion?'

I told her about Alex's move. 'That's not all. John's popped the question. Mum said yes. We're going to move off the estate.'

She made all the right noises about my news.

'Wait here,' she said. 'I'm going to get ready. I'll be ten minutes.'

I didn't see the trail bike or the rider watching us from a distance. I climbed the steps to the multiplex with Abi by my side. It was part of the retail park.

I paid for the tickets while Abi bought popcorn. We showed our tickets to the attendant. Neither of us looked back. We didn't see Jason Leather asking a member of staff what time the film finished.

We left the cinema the same way, carefree, oblivious to the shadowy figures that had begun to detach themselves from the corner of the bowling alley and Pizza Hut. Our bus was approaching the stop so we started to run. Ours weren't the only footsteps that echoed in the frosty air. I heard them and turned. I cursed under my breath.

Abi shot a startled glance my way. 'What is it?'

'Them.'

Jamie and Dean had just stepped out in front of us. Three more gang members came up behind us. Mitch was one of them.

'Good film?' Jamie asked.

I didn't grace the comment with an answer. 'What do you want?'

'Nothing much,' Jamie drawled. 'I just thought I'd touch base with you, you know, catch up on things, chew the fat.'

Abi was nervous. Her hand slipped into mine. Jason was standing right up close, his breath on her neck. I tried to pull her to me.

'Your brother's got plenty to say for himself,' Jamie observed. 'The way I hear it, he's been shooting his mouth off, saying I can't touch him.'

'You can't. Not anymore.'

I said it as firmly as I could to conceal the quiver in my voice. I closed my fingers round Abi's hand by way of reassurance. She was cold. Her touch was ice.

'Poor Ethan,' Jamie said. 'You don't still believe in happy endings, do you?'

Something in the way he looked at me made my blood

run cold. Mitch grabbed me from behind. Jason helped restrain me. Simultaneously, Jamie pulled Abi close.

'Don't,' she said, ducking her head away from his warm breath.

He put his finger to her lips. 'Shh.'

He made a show of looking her up and down.

I was struggling to break free. 'Get away from her!'

Jamie traced a line down her throat. He took the zip of her jacket between finger and thumb. The zip hissed down and he slid his hand inside. Tears spilled from her eyes.

Jamie pressed his hand against her breast and turned to look at me. 'It would be a shame if anything happened to her.'

I twisted and strained to get free.

'I can get to Alex any time I want,' Jamie said. 'I can get to you and your slapper of a mother … and I can get to her.' He closed his eyes and nodded. 'Mm. She feels *good*.'

He kept his hand on Abi for a few moments. Then he zipped up her jacket, patted her face and laughed out loud.

'You know what, boys, I think I was getting her excited.'

I finally twisted free and threw a punch, stumbling in my haste to get to him. Dean stuck out a leg and sent me sprawling. The Tribe strode away laughing. Jamie left us with something to think about.

'Still living at number sixteen, Abi? I might call round sometime.'

I scrambled to my feet and brushed her hair from her face.

'I'm so sorry, Abi.'

She didn't speak. Her eyes said everything. I thumbed a number in my mobile.

'Mum, it's me. Listen, I ran into Jamie Leather. No, nothing happened. Just stop talking, will you? This is urgent.' He had her attention. 'Call the prison now. I think they're going to do something to Alex.'

I cut the call and held Abi.

'I won't let them touch you.'

Her attempt at bravery crumbled and she sobbed against my shoulder.

'What can you do, Ethan? They're not afraid of you. They're not afraid of the police. They can do anything they like.'

I stroked her hair. 'No matter what I have to do, I'm going to protect you.' My mind was racing. I knew there was a way out. 'They'll never put their filthy hands on you ever again.'

Jamie Leather didn't make empty threats. That night three inmates cornered Alex and beat him so savagely he had to be rushed to hospital. In the early hours of the morning Mum and I were at his bedside keeping vigil over him. I stared down at Alex's face. It was barely recognisable. Mitch had his wish.

There were swellings all over Alex's face and head. There were different coloured bruises marking his face. His eyes were swollen shut. He was on a ventilator. He had a thick tube in his mouth attached to a machine. It was tied in place with tape. He had a tube up his right nostril hanging loose. Two more lines went into his body. We had been there about an hour when the doctor asked to speak to Mum privately. He said Alex should make a full recovery.

Should.

She returned torn between misery and relief.

'They could have killed him, Ethan,' Mum wept. 'My son, your brother, they could have killed him.'

I put my arm round her shoulders. She buried her face into my chest.

'When's it going to end? What are we going to do?'

What could I say? Too much had been said already. I had to act. Mum glanced up at me.

'Why don't you take a break?' She fumbled in her handbag. 'Here, get yourself a drink. See if John wants to come in and sit with me.'

I found John standing by a window, gazing across the grounds of the hospital. 'She wants you.'

He nodded. 'I'll go in a minute. How's she taking it?'

'What do you think?'

'What about you, Ethan? Are you OK?'

That question again. Everybody asked it. John put his hands on my shoulders. 'I'm going to get you and your mum off that estate,' he said.

'Good plan,' I said, 'but you can't get Alex out of prison. Jamie will wait until he's better, then he'll find a way to get to him again. It will never be over. How do we protect him?'

'What are you saying, Ethan?'

I couldn't say too much. So I didn't.

'I don't know, maybe that life's not fair.'

I went outside. There were flakes of snow in the air. I stepped into the darkness, turning my collar up against the cold. I remembered the way Jamie had touched Abi. I thought of Alex lying in intensive care. Finally, I recalled the way Jamie laughed in the face of the law. I could hear

Alex's voice in my head, telling me that I was weak. I pulled out my mobile and made a call.

'It's me.' I listened to the voice at the other end. 'That's right, I'm ready.'

My fingers trembled as I slipped the mobile back in my pocket.

It wasn't the cold.

PART THREE

A NIGHT OF FIRE

19

A light seemed to have gone out in Abi. She was forever looking for somebody in the shadows. She didn't like being on her own. She hid what had happened from her parents, but they sensed something was wrong.

'You've got to stop being afraid,' I told her. 'It'll pass.'

'How, Ethan? How will it pass? Do you think Jamie Leather is going to let go? Oh, he'll let it go quiet now and then. That's part of it. He wants to keep us guessing. But he isn't going to stop.' She dropped her voice. 'He touched me. I can still feel it. He put his hand on me. It makes my skin crawl.'

Every word was an accusation. I did my best to reassure her, but what words could I offer without giving myself away?

'You've got to trust me. I won't let him come near you ever again.'

'You keep saying that. What can you do, Ethan? Jamie put your brother in intensive care. He was in a prison and nobody was able to protect him.' She let the words sink in. 'Tell me, how can you take care of me? You can't even help yourself. You can't save your family. Jamie Leather is above the law.'

I walked her to the house. I slipped my arms round her.

'Forget about Jamie.'

She tried to speak, but I pressed a finger to her lips.

'Do you trust me?'

'Of course, but ...'

'No buts, Abi. I'm telling you people like Jamie, they make enemies. All the things they've done, they come back to haunt them. It was the same with Carl Nash. He seemed invincible. It's going to happen to Jamie, maybe not today or even tomorrow, but it will happen. Don't you see that?'

She murmured an uncertain reply.

'Yes.'

'Jamie is making too many enemies. He's on his way out.'

She seemed wary of something in my voice. I left her outside her house. As I walked away I had a knot of frustration in my gut. I was about to turn towards home when I got a text. I jogged across the road and took a left. I stopped in the cul-de-sac and looked around. An Audi A3 appeared and flashed its headlights. I got in. The ground seemed to lurch under my feet. This was it.

'When?'

Darren popped in a stick of chewing gum. I registered Simmo's presence in the back seat. It looked like he'd worked his way up. I had seen him broken and friendless. Now he was Darren's right-hand man. That was something I noticed about Simmo. All the beatings he'd taken, he always seemed to come back punching. He was a survivor.

'I'll tell you when we're ready,' Darren said. 'Sorry about your brother, by the way.'

I looked straight ahead.

'No, you're not. You did the same to Mitch. You and Jamie, you're not that different.'

'Maybe, but I'm the only one who can do anything for your brother. I've got Tattoo Man. But nothing comes for free. There's always a price tag attached.'

'And this is the world you live in?'

'Welcome to Scumville.'

'At least cut the crap about feeling any sympathy,' I told him. 'There's only one reason we're sitting here.'

'That's right,' Darren agreed. 'It's business. That's the way it is in this world. You do what you have to do.'

'Right. We all do what we have to do.' I waited a beat then turned to look at him. I couldn't believe I was in the car with him, planning something like this. 'What you said about waiting until you're ready, it's not good enough. When do you produce Tattoo Man?'

'Stop stressing. It's in hand.'

'I need to know details.'

'It's not going to happen, Ethan. I run this firm. Nobody else.'

Out of the corner of my eye I registered Simmo's change of expression. He still wanted to be top dog.

'You're best knowing nothing until you're needed,' Darren continued, oblivious. He glanced at my hands. 'You're shaking. That's no good.'

What did he expect? Sure, I'd been on the edge of his world for years, but I wasn't part of it. I wasn't meant to be here. But it was the only way I could get any kind of justice.

'I'll be OK.'

'You'd better be.'

I tried to control the shakes.

'Can't you tell me anything?'

'Listen,' Darren said. 'Jamie's got what he wants, for now at least. He knows he's stronger than me. He's got more soldiers.'

Simmo said nothing.

'Jamie's made an example of Alex. He thinks nobody can touch him.'

'They can't.'

'That's where you're wrong, Ethan. Jamie Leather has a weakness. It's his arrogance. Sometime soon he will drop his guard. An opportunity will come along. We're going to let him think he's fireproof.' He made a gun with his fingers and thumb. 'Then we do him.'

The gesture stayed in my mind. The hand would be mine. The squeeze on the trigger. Mine. The responsibility. All mine. We spent several moments scanning the street. There was nothing to say. He decided it was time I left.

'Stay strong, yeah.' He made a joke. 'Have yourself a merry little Christmas. Then in the New Year ... well, I don't need to spell it out, do I?'

Simmo gave the street the once-over then tapped on the window.

'OK, move.'

I had only gone a few steps when Darren shouted a parting shot out of the window.

'And get over those shakes.'

I had to wait until mid-February for Darren's plan to bear fruit. It was a Wednesday afternoon. I was lying on the settee talking to Abi on my mobile when I heard Mum scream. I stumbled to the door and pounded downstairs.

'What's wrong?'

'There's nothing wrong.'

Her eyes were bright with joy. She was holding a letter in her right hand.

'Read it.'

It was everything Darren had promised. He had produced Tattoo Man. Alex had his appeal.

'That's brilliant. He's coming home, Mum.'

She was trembling.

'I don't want to get my hopes up.'

'He's made a full recovery from his injuries. Now he's got his appeal. It's just a matter of time. He's coming home.'

She read the letter again and again, scrutinising every line.

'It's real,' I said. 'The words aren't going to fade.'

She nodded absent-mindedly. 'They've found a witness. It's got to be Alex's Tattoo Man. I'd started to think he didn't exist. I'm going to call the solicitor. The letter says I should get in touch if I have any questions.'

I watched her make the call. She hung up and filled in the details.

'This witness, this Tattoo Man, it seems he was working away. Soon after he got back, he heard what happened at the trial and went to the police.'

She waited for me to say something. I didn't.

'That's not all,' she said. 'It appears there's more new evidence. You know the two men who testified against Alex?'

'The ones in the bar?'

'Right, the ones in the bar. Well, one of them was seen two miles away at the time of the fight. We can prove he lied on oath.'

I heard her out. I wondered why she hadn't remarked on the coincidence of one witness turning up at the very moment the others had their testimony called into question. Darren Nash was thorough. I had to give him that. The prosecution case had just taken a hit beneath the water line. Darren had kept his side of the bargain. Now I had to keep mine. Oblivious to the thoughts running through my mind, Mum made another call.

'I'm going to tell John.'

I listened as she stumbled through the excited explanation, then I walked over to the window. The sun was going down. I could hardly breathe.

The hand on the trigger.

Mine.

The responsibility.

Mine.

It had to be soon.

I opened the door.

'Are you home, Mum? Abi's with me.'

It was a week since we'd got the news about the appeal. We found Mum in the living room. She had her mobile in her hand. She was smiling.

'Hi, Abi.'

Abi smiled a hello.

'Who was that?' I asked, nodding at the phone in her hand.

'The solicitor.'

'Good news?'

'Yes. Yes, I think so.' She looked at me for the first time. 'She's had a meeting with Tattoo Man. He's a credible witness. Seems he left the area immediately after the fight. He was taking up a job offer. He didn't even know Alex had been charged. That's why he took so long to come forward.'

I listened. The blood thudded in my head. I didn't comment. I knew exactly what was behind Tattoo Man's reappearance.

'What about the witnesses in the bar?'

'One is placed somewhere else at the time. The other one has gone missing.'

She glanced at her watch. 'Look, I've got to get ready for work. John's picking me up in half an hour.' She kissed me on the cheek. 'You've been my rock, Ethan. I don't know what I would have done without you.'

She left the room. I stared after her.

'What's wrong?' Abi asked.

'Why's something got to be wrong?'

'You don't fool me, Ethan. Do I need to be scared?'

'There's nothing to be scared of, Abi. Nothing.'

But there was plenty to be scared of. You think Hell is some place deep underground, but it isn't. It's the other side of the living room wall. It's in the eyes of the men and women you know. It's in the tiniest of actions that can change your life. Mum's words haunted me. I was her rock. Why did she have to say that? I closed my eyes. Just for a moment I dreamed that it was possible to pull back from the fire. But I was going to get burned.

'Ethan?'

Abi's voice brought me back to the present.

'What's bothering you?'

I drew her close.
'It's nothing.'
Nothing at all.

20

Mitch had become Tribe through and through. He was there when it started. He was there when the estate caught fire. He was there when a routine stop and search turned into a night nobody would ever forget. Jamie was driving, Jason in front, Mitch in the back. He stopped the car.

'It's just a stop and search,' he said. 'Leave the talking to me. They're not going to find anything.'

Mitch tried to hiss a warning. 'Jamie, there's something you should know.'

Ignoring him, Jamie wound the window down.

'Yes, officer.'

Mitch fell back against the seat, fingernails clawing at the upholstery.

'Would you like to step out of the car, sir?'

Jamie winked.

'What are you stopping us for?' he asked as he got out.

'We have reason to believe this vehicle has been used to transport Class A drugs.'

Jamie chuckled. 'This one? Somebody's been feeding you bum information.'

Mitch wound the window down and tried to catch Jamie's eye.

'I'm PC Phil Jevons,' the officer said. 'This is PC Michael Smith.'

A second car pulled up. There were more introductions. The stop and search was attracting a small crowd.

'Is this your vehicle, sir?'

Jamie's gaze wandered round the four cops.

'Two cars? You must think you're onto something. Somebody's been talking to you. Who is it?'

PC Jevons told Jamie all the information he was obliged to give: his name and station, the law under which he had stopped the car, why he had been stopped and searched and what they were looking for. Mitch was still trying to attract Jamie's attention.

'What's your name, sir?'

Somebody in the watching crowd shouted the answer.

'This copper doesn't know who you are, Jamie.'

Jamie grinned. 'He knows.' He caught Jevons' eye. 'We're old friends aren't we, Phil? You're just doing your duty, aren't you *officer*?'

Jevons remained deadpan. He had been one of the arresting officers when Jamie assaulted Simmo. Jamie gave his name, address and date of birth. Mitch was looking more agitated than ever. When the police weren't looking he opened his palm then closed it again. He was holding a plastic wrap. Just for a moment Jamie's face tightened. While he was being searched he fixed Mitch with a stare. Mitch took it as an order to run. He threw open the door and set off across the road. Immediately, two of the officers gave chase and brought him down. The crowd started to shout.

'Leave him alone!'

'Yes, get your hands off him!'

That's when the first missile was thrown. A half brick smashed the side window of one of the police vehicles. PC Jevons shouted something. The crowd was still growing. Those at the back were egging on the ones at the front. Another half brick flew, then a volley of stones. Stop and searches were a regular event on the Green. Most times nobody paid any attention. But something was happening that night. All the suppressed anger, all the hopelessness, the whole sense of decay and decline on the estate seemed to come together in a moment of rage. The sight of Mitch on the ground being restrained made it boil over.

'Let him go!' somebody shouted.

Mitch started to struggle. He was yelling and fighting back. Boys pulled scarves across faces, tightened hoods, flexed fingers inside woollen gloves. They reached for bottles, cans, stones, anything to hurl at the police. The missiles were drumming on the two cars. A brick thumped through the windscreen of PC Jevons' car and a huge roar went up.

Jevons tried to address the crowd. More kids were coming, some as young as twelve or thirteen. They were running, scrambling over walls, leaping up and down, punching fists in the air. A small protest was turning into a revolt. The driver of the second car grabbed his sleeve.

'We've lost the crowd, Phil. We don't have the manpower to deal with these numbers. We've got to get out of here.'

Seeing the state of Jevons' car, the four of them

scrambled into the second vehicle and roared away. Boys rushed forward to kick at the retreating cops. More missiles rained down. There were up to fifty people, mostly young. As one police car sped away the crowd turned its anger on the abandoned vehicle. Within moments it was lying on its side. Somebody torched the petrol tank. Flames leapt, highlighting faces in the dusk. Smoke billowed across the estate.

Jamie marched over to Mitch and cuffed him across the head. 'Are you insane? I said no drugs. Which bit do you not understand?' He stared at the boys dancing round the blazing car. 'Look what you've started.'

Mitch rubbed his head. 'They chased the coppers away, didn't they?'

Jamie watched the scene for a few moments then grinned. 'Yes, did you see those piggies run?'

Half a mile across the estate Simmo took a call.

'That right?'

He held the phone out to Darren.

'I think you want to hear this.'

Darren listened. One of his soldiers was on a trail bike, following Jamie. He saw the stop and search and the developing riot.

'There's how many?' Darren asked. 'A hundred! Where did they come from?' He listened to the rest of the report. 'And there's a cop car on fire? Oh, this just gets better. The Beast are going to have their hands full tonight.' He finally saw the drifting smoke and thought for a moment or two. 'Is Jamie still there? You did good. Stay on him. Don't let him out of your sight.' He glanced at Simmo. 'This is it. It's the perfect opportunity.'

'It's risky,' Simmo said. 'Crowds are unpredictable. A riot isn't something you can control.'

'Who says I want to control it? I couldn't if I wanted to. No, let the good times roll. This is going to tie the coppers up all night. It's our chance.'

He thought for a moment.

'I know how to separate him from his boys. Don't look so serious, Simmo. It's show time. Jamie Leather's toast.'

He started texting.

I was at Abi's when I got it. She saw me reading Darren's text.

'Who's that?'

I stood up. I was a sleep-walker. None of this was real.

'I said—'

'I heard. Don't worry about it.'

'Don't tell me what to think, Ethan. What's wrong?'

I turned my back on her.

'Look, I've got to go.'

'You're not leaving,' she said. 'I won't let you.' She scrambled off the settee and put her arms round me. 'Why don't you say something, Ethan? You're scaring me.'

I peeled her fingers from my neck. I was scaring myself.

'Ethan!'

I stopped at the door, but I didn't look back.

'I love you, Abi.'

Abi laid the flat of her hand on the door so it slammed shut.

'Tell me who made that call, Ethan. Talk to me.'

'Leave it,' I said.

I opened the door again, stepped into the gathering darkness and set off across the estate. A sense of loss enveloped me. I was walking away from a future that could be beautiful.

'Ethan! Don't talk down to me! I deserve to know.'

I pulled her to me. I knew the feel of her, the smell of her so well. Too well. How could I risk losing her? Then I remembered Jamie's threats.

'I wish I could tell you.'

'Why does everything feel like a goodbye, Ethan? What have you got yourself into?'

It was killing me to shut her out.

'I can't say.'

'It's got something to do with Alex, hasn't it?'

Her hands flew to my face. The slender fingers traced every feature as if committing me to memory. She kissed me and there was desperation in her kiss.

'Turn round, Ethan. Come back to the house. Whatever it is, we can sort it out.'

'Abi, you have no idea.'

A car swept by, tyres roaring on the tarmac.

'It's Jamie Leather, isn't it? We've got dreams, Ethan. You, me, university, a flat in a new town. We can have a whole new life. Please Ethan, don't throw it all away.' She slapped her palms against my chest. 'Talk to me. Be honest with me! You can't just stand there, giving me nothing. I'm trying to help.'

A thought came into my head.

'Do you really want to help?'

'You know I do.'

'I want you to find somewhere to go, just for an hour.'

A look of confusion crossed her face.

'What?'

'Don't go home. Walk around. Anything. If anybody

asks, you were with me until half past seven. No, eight o'clock's better.'

Her eyes flashed.

'What are you saying?'

'I'm asking you to give me an alibi.'

This time there was revulsion in her voice.

'What the hell are you going to do?'

'You know what my family's been through. I'm going to put an end to it.'

She took a step back.

'Abi?'

Her voice was suddenly hoarse, indignation fighting with the need to whisper. 'You want me to lie for you?'

I turned and walked away. I could feel her eyes on my back.

She called after me. 'You can't ask me to do this. This isn't love. It's wrong. You're using me.'

I didn't look back. It was too late for love.

I stopped by the Aldi car park. It was empty and the shutters were pulled down over the windows. There was the thunder of truncheons beating on riot shields in the distance. Petrol bombs were cutting blazing tracks in the sky.

'Raining fire,' I murmured, remembering a child's words, a child's world years before.

I reached the lock-up, a garage at the back of the Parade, and rapped on the door. Simmo let me in. He slapped a key into my palm.

'Good luck, Ethan,' he said. 'I wish you weren't the one. You're the only person who ever tried to help me.'

I examined the steel shelves and their array of motor

parts. There were oily tarpaulins, invoices, three pairs of overalls, two blue, one green. It was all a matter of waiting for Darren's text. It would tell me where to find Jamie. Then I would finish the job. Darren had told me to sort out my hands. I looked at them. The shakes were worse than ever. I knew the truth about myself if nobody else did. I wasn't a gunman. I was a scared kid. But I had to make myself into an iceman. I had to find the steel to carry it through.

For Alex.

I unwrapped the weapon. I had been expecting the Agram machine pistol, Darren's weapon of choice. Instead I was looking at a Walther PPK, the same kind of gun Jamie had offered me on Bonfire night two years ago. I had refused it then. Now I had no choice.

I stood in the half-light. I felt dizzy, light-headed. It was as if I had picked up Alex's life where he had left it when he went inside. I felt an unexpected calm. Though there was sweat on my forehead and on my top lip, though my fingers trembled when I held them out, I knew I had to go ahead with it. I had to suppress the waves of panic that still rushed over me at regular intervals. I had to pick up the weapon, squeeze the trigger, take a life. That's what lay behind the dizziness. I had climbed to a place few people on the estate would ever be.

I was going to kill.

Those boys in their black jackets and scarves called themselves soldiers because they bore arms. I didn't buy it. Having a gun in your hand doesn't make you a soldier. I refused to honour the squalid, pointless crime I was about to commit with any kind of justification. There would be no parades to commemorate it, no flags, no bugle calls. It would be remembered the only way that was appropriate, with condemnation and the washing of hands. It was necessary. It was as simple as that. I didn't look for good to come out of his lonely mission, only closure.

I thought of Abi. I couldn't forget the look in her eyes when I'd asked her to give me an alibi. It was beyond horror. It was as if all the love she had felt for me had turned to acid and burned through her soul. In that moment her trust in me had died.

I smiled grimly at the final irony. She didn't even know what I had planned. Maybe she thought it was a beating. She knew about the baseball bat in the cupboard. She would know the truth soon enough. I weighed the gun in my gloved hand.

Was it possible, even now, to put the gun down, to walk out of the door locking it behind me and pick up the pieces of my life? I turned the idea over in my mind and saw it for what it was: a grotesque lie. Jamie was like an infectious disease. He would never let go. I remembered everything Darren had told me. I checked the safety and shoved the weapon in my jacket.

Screw you, Jamie.

Jamie Leather was on the scene. He watched from a distance, winding down the Subaru's window and staring at the mayhem. About eighty rioters had detached themselves from the main crowd. They were streaming across the perimeter road and making for the retail park. Some seized shopping trolleys from the bays at the supermarket. Others were already trying to smash their way into the Next store and Foot Locker. They ran at the large windows and started kicking. The assault was rhythmic, almost choreographed. One boy saw the police watching from a distance. He strode forward, gesturing.

'See what we're doing? We're taking anything we want.' He laughed. 'What are you going to do about it?'

Outnumbered, the police looked on helplessly.

'I didn't give permission for all this,' Jamie grunted. 'What's this got to do with the stop and search?'

The smoke stung his eyes. Suddenly there was a power on the estate he was unable to exploit or command.

'This hasn't got anything to do with what happened earlier,' Mitch answered. 'This is what you call spontaneous.'

Jamie showed what he thought of spontaneous revolt. He spat on the pavement.

'When this is over, I'm going to be calling on a few people. Nothing happens without my say-so.'

Mitch watched the kids smashing their way into the shops. 'Try telling them that.'

That's when Jamie's phone buzzed. He read the text and frowned.

'I've got to go.'

'Need company?'

The frown was still there.

'No, this is personal. Keep an eye on this. See if there's anything in it for us.'

Jamie would have been very interested in a conversation taking place half a mile away. Darren Nash was at the wheel of his Rav 4. There was somebody Jamie knew sitting in the passenger seat. Darren's secret weapon. He handed her phone back.

'Thanks for the lend, Lindsay. Leather has no idea what's coming to him.'

Lindsay Clarke looked uncomfortable. She darted anxious glances up and down the street, picked at her skirt.

'What are you going to do to him?'

'There's nothing to worry about,' Darren said with a chuckle. 'By the time Jamie answers the call, you and I will be long gone.'

'I don't like it.'

'Stop worrying. Everybody's at the riot. They're having a party. You should see them. They're like moths round a light bulb. They emptied Superdrug. One kid had a box of Imodium.' He thought that was funny. 'But that's not where the real action is this evening.'

'You've got to keep my name out of this,' Lindsay asked. 'Jamie would kill me.'

'You've nothing to worry about. I won't grass you up.'

Lindsay wanted to believe.

'And the money?'

Darren handed her a roll of notes bound by an elastic band. Lindsay reached for the door handle.

'Aren't you going to count it?' Darren asked.

Lindsay scrambled out of the car.

'There's no need.'

As she tottered away on killer heels, Darren laughed out loud. He'd never seen anyone so keen to escape from his vehicle. He watched her cute little walk for a few moments then he read the text. Sending it from Lindsay's phone was an act of genius if he said so himself. He laughed again.

Perfect.

I had my eyes on Jamie. He had just pulled up opposite the Beehive. He lowered the window and called into the night.

'Lindsay?'

He kept the engine running. The car filled with the smell of burning. Smoke from the riot was spiralling in the beam of the headlights.

'Don't play games,' he said. 'I know you're there. What's this about?'

It was darker than usual. The pub had its shutters down like every one of the remaining businesses on the estate. The moment the trouble started all the premises in a mile radius shut up shop.

I tried to imagine the damage the bullet would do. A shot to the head. There would be blood, bone fragments, a mess of brain and body fluids. It was as if I was standing on the edge of a deep well. It was full of horror.

'Lindsay?'

Darren, Simmo and all the main players would be standing on the frontline, getting their faces on the police video footage. Who better than the boys in blue to give them an alibi? I made my move. I didn't see the bottle until I stumbled over it. It rolled across the pavement and dropped into the gutter. Jamie squinted through the murk created by the smoke and the evening mist. He took a step forward. I shrank into the shadows, barely able to breathe.

'Lindsay?' He couldn't see me 'Linds?' He grew suspicious. 'Who is that?'

I tugged the balaclava down over my face. There must be no mistakes this time. I stole round behind him. He was still calling Lindsay's name when I put the muzzle to his temple. The horror was bubbling out of the well.

'Not bad,' Jamie grunted. 'I didn't hear a thing after the bottle. Good recovery, man.'

I didn't answer.

'Are you alone?' he asked.

I said nothing.

'It's you, isn't it, Darren?'

Still nothing.

'Where are you going to do it?' Jamie asked. 'Not here. It's too busy. There might be witnesses.'

He was bluffing. At the first sign of trouble, the pub had put the shutters up for the evening and the frontline was hundreds of metres away on the far side of the Parade.

'What are you going to do, take me for a ride and show me all the bad things I've done in my life?' He chuckled. 'What's this? A Christmas Carol with a bullet at the end?'

That's when he did it. He started to walk away from me. I found my voice.

'Stay where you are.'

Jamie froze. He turned and stared. 'Ethan. Oh, this is priceless. NSC are gambling on some angry kid. They must be desperate. You're not up to this, you know. Popping a guy isn't like reading a book.'

I had blood pounding in my head. In spite of the night chill there was sweat gluing my shirt to my skin.

'It's not going to look good on your CV, you know. So you're Darren's boy now.'

In spite of myself, I heard my breath catch. He sensed weakness. It made him smile.

'That's a tasty piece you're holding. Same as the one I showed you once. Go on,' he said, 'shoot.'

247

I took a long, shuddering breath. I couldn't do it.

'Tell you what,' Jamie said. 'I'll make it easy for you.'

He closed his eyes and pressed his forehead against the barrel of the Walther. He held out his arms in mock crucifixion.

'I'm not looking. That should make it easy for you. Go on, tough guy. Pull the trigger.'

I didn't fire. I couldn't. I was numb. Jamie's eyes snapped open. They were hard with contempt. He pushed the gun to one side and pointed a finger in my face.

'You're just like your brother. You're pathetic.'

I spoke for the first time in over a minute.

'Just because we're not killers like you doesn't make us weak.'

I realised what I'd said. We're not killers. That was when I knew for certain. It hadn't been just a moment's hesitation. How could I have ever thought I would pull the trigger? Suddenly I just wanted to get rid of the weapon. I lowered it from his face. Jamie laughed at me. 'You don't have the guts.'

He made a grab for the gun. So I let him have it. I smashed the grip in his face so hard my fist screamed. Blood spurted from ripped flesh. Then I walked away. I put the safety on and tossed the gun aside. It landed on the ground with a dull thud. It wasn't a conscious decision, just an instinctive need. It barely occurred to me that I would have to pay for what I'd done. I had more pressing concerns. Jamie was clawing his way unsteadily to his feet.

Glimpsing movement, I felt my neck start to prickle. He could pick it up and shoot me in the back any time he wanted. Somehow I kept on walking even when he called my name. I pulled off the balaclava and gloves and tossed them into the flames that were licking around the wall at the back of the Parade. Stripped of the assassin's uniform, I fled into the night. I was done with the gun.

21

But the gun wasn't done with me.

Darren left it a day or two. He knew where to find me. The car prowled along the pavement and pulled in. Simmo got out of the passenger seat and slipped into the back. Darren did the talking.

'Get in the car, Ethan.'

Did Simmo shake his head? I glanced at him and remembered what he'd said in the lock-up.

I wish you weren't the one.

But I was. I had thrown away the gun. I was half expecting to be delivered to some secluded spot for a beating. Or worse. A kind of numb, helpless horror chewed away at me. Darren twisted in the driver's seat. His face was white with suppressed fury. 'Are you crazy? I came through for you, didn't I Ethan?'

He watched the automaton nod.

'Yes, that's right. I kept my part of the bargain.' He jabbed a finger into my face. 'So what do you do? You turn chicken. You even throw the gun away.'

Darren heard my silence and flicked a glance at Simmo in the back.

'Do you believe this guy?' he snorted. 'Jamie could come after it and off me with my own piece. Unbelievable. He doesn't even say sorry.'

I managed to force out an answer. 'It wouldn't do much good, would it?'

The white-hot glare was back on me. He had hold of my hair and slammed my head against the side window. My cheek slid on the cold, moist glass.

'Something tells me you're not taking this seriously.'

My ears rang.

'I'm listening, Darren. What do I say?'

'That isn't up to me, is it? You blew it, Ethan. I give you everything and what do you give me? A big fat zero in return.' He let go and watched the street. 'You get nothing for nothing. There's got to be payback, Ethan, with interest.'

'What do you want?'

'Right now?' Darren said. 'Nothing. Thanks to you, this whole thing's a complete mess. There's some sorting out to do. I've got Lindsay holed up in a safe house and she's terrified of what Jamie's going to do to her. She's screaming about police protection, for crying out loud!'

He rubbed at his face as if trying to scrub it clean of problems.

'Get out. Get the hell out of my car!'

I scrambled out of the passenger seat, grateful that I could walk away after what I'd done. He leaned forward to look at me.

'This isn't over, Ethan. You're going to pay me back and, believe me, I'm going to demand a high price. I'm going to make you crawl over broken glass for causing me so much grief. Now get out of my sight.'

Alex walked free a week later. He returned to an estate where everything was the same, but everything had changed. The houses looked just like they had when he went away. The Parade was the same bleak, wind-scoured relic of better times. There were fewer shops than when he had left. Two of the looted businesses closed for good. Mr Khan was made of stronger stuff. The 24/7 was open the morning after the riots. The retail park reopened at the end of the week. When the rioters are done yelling, money still talks.

There were just as many people out of work, just as many who were lonely, rejected, marginalised, betrayed. There was the same number of kids hanging round on street corners, waiting for the police to move them on. The gangs were still preparing for war. The gun was still there.

As Alex walked through the door and dropped his bag on the table, he didn't care about any of this. He didn't want to know. He wasn't stupid enough to believe all his problems would just go away, but he wasn't ready to face reality, not yet. There is a time, after some great trauma, when the mere absence of pain is something to be cherished.

For now, he was content to live in a bubble of hope and illusion. He just wanted to feel the familiarity of home, its warmth, its safety. He wanted it to be perfect, inviolate. He walked from room to room acclimatising himself with the place he had missed so much. I watched him, wondering when he was going to ask how I got him out and what price was to be paid. Mum stood at the bottom of the stairs and listened.

'Do you think he's all right?'

He was fine. He'd just walked free from a living nightmare. He was learning how to live again.

'Give him time, eh?'

'He's acting strange.'

'Don't you think you'd be out of kilter if you'd spent the last few months in a prison cell? It isn't a normal place.'

Tears spilled down Mum's cheeks. She palmed them away and confided in me.

'You know when we were waiting for the trial, I used to go up and watch him sleeping. I knew they were going to take my little boy away. I just wanted to keep him safe.'

She placed a hand on my shoulder.

'There were moments when I thought we were never going to get him home.' She let out a long, shuddering breath. 'It's been a terrible time, but it's coming to an end. We're moving into the new house soon. Then we will never have to look at this place ever again.'

I nodded absent-mindedly. The Green still had its claws in me. Darren's words kept ringing in my ears. If she thought we were looking down on the promised land, she was fooling herself.

Alex came down from his room.

'Nobody in?'

'Mum and John are down the house,' I told him. 'You know, getting things ready for the move. You OK?'

He nodded. 'Everything feels kind of strange.'

We talked for a while, stuff about the past, stuff about

the future. We had our dreams. For Alex it was pride in his work. For me it was football. The dreams fell apart, but we were still standing. For now. It was time to get things straight between us.

'I can't forget your face when you heard I'd turned down Darren's offer. Do you hate me for it?'

He looked at me as if I'd just grown two heads.

'Of course I don't hate you, Ethan. Forget it; I never wanted you to go out on a limb for me. I'm the one who did wrong.' He sat down opposite me. 'You were right about me all along.'

My heart kicked. 'Meaning?'

'Look, this is the only time I am ever going to talk about it. I was there when Jamie popped Carl Nash.'

He saw the way I stared.

'Yes, I know, I've denied it long enough. I watched it happen, Ethan. I'm not proud of myself. I stood by while Jamie killed Carl. Once we got him away, I helped wash him down with petrol, you know, get rid of the evidence. It was wrong, but I still went along with it. It's hard to explain. I was sleep-walking. Do you understand that?'

I understood in a way he couldn't imagine.

'It was self-defence that night in the Beehive,' he said, 'but that doesn't make me innocent. When it comes to the greatest crime of all, I'm guilty Ethan, guilty as hell.'

'You didn't kill Carl,' I reminded him. 'Jamie did.'

'I didn't do anything to stop him. I have to live with that.'

The wind boomed against the panes. It was time for me to tell my story.

'You're not the only one with things to get off his chest.'

Alex heard something in my voice and leaned forward.

'What are you talking about?'

'I went after Jamie.'

There was a long silence. He stared as if he didn't recognise me as his brother.

'Went after him how?'

'I took Darren's gun. He wanted me to do Jamie. I said yes.'

'Tell me you're making it up.'

His eyes were willing me to backtrack, but I couldn't undo the past and I wasn't going to lie.

'I went looking for him just like I said. I had the gun to his head.'

He let air out between his teeth.

'I couldn't pull the trigger.'

Alex looked at me and saw a stranger. I told my story, every squalid, little detail. He didn't say a word. He held my eyes with his own silent stare.

'Mum doesn't get to know about this. We've put her through enough.'

'Who's arguing?' Silence prowled around us a while. 'Looks like I've made two enemies. Word is, Jamie wants revenge for what I did.'

'He'll be after blood,' Alex said, his voice low. 'It's an obsession with Jamie. If somebody makes him look bad, he just keeps hunting him down. You don't know what you've done.'

'I understand consequences. You don't know the half of it, Alex. Darren came looking for me too. He's going to want his pound of flesh.'

Alex pinched the bridge of his nose. 'It takes a special kind of genius to make enemies of the Tribe *and* NSC. How the hell do we get out of this one?'

'I don't know.'

He got up and walked to the door. On his way past he rested a hand on my shoulder.

'Me neither.'

A day went by. Two. I lived on my nerves and wondered when Jamie would pay me a visit. Or Darren. I discovered how it had been for Alex, always on edge, never at peace with himself. Now it was my turn to walk the razor's edge. How could I have a future? One wanted me dead. The other was calling in a debt of blood. Of course, I patched things up with Abi. She thought it had all been talk, the night I went after Jamie. Nothing happened. Somehow she convinced herself that nothing was ever meant to happen.

Abi.

My Abi.

When I think what I did. When I remember how I put her in harm's way. I was wrong. So wrong.

I heard the doorbell. I was home alone. We had been at the new house all day decorating. I was going out with Abi later, so I had to come back home for a shower. I had taken to checking who was at the front door before I opened it. I peered through the blinds. There was a surprise waiting for me. I don't even know why I opened the door to him. I held it ajar, checking the street.

'Mitch? What the hell do you want?'

He stood with the dusk behind him.

'Things have been bad between us, Ethan. Can we talk?'

I stepped back to let him in. That was my first mistake.

'I'm going out. Abi's on her way. She'll be here any moment.'

'You really care for her, don't you?'

I should have known then. The way he said it. Like an idiot, I let him in. I was aware of the dark life in his eyes. They roved round the room then they fixed me with a cold look of appraisal. How could I have imagined there was even a scrap of trust left between us? He didn't remember friendship. He remembered betrayal.

'So what's this about?'

'I wanted to put something to rest,' he said. 'I don't blame you anymore, Ethan.'

He came out with it. Just like that. Deadpan. There was no emotion, just a statement of fact. I wondered if it was something he'd learned off by heart.

'That right?' I said.

I wasn't in any mood for reconciliation.

'I was ashamed for a long time because of what happened to you, Mitch. I felt as if I had betrayed you.'

'Sounds like there's a but coming.'

'Have you forgotten the night outside the cinema? You had hold of me while Jamie put his hands all over Abi. I think you could say we're quits. I don't have any trouble looking you in the eye. I haven't felt guilty in a while.'

Mitch considered my words. 'Sounds like there's nothing more to say.'

There was a moment's silence.

'Before I go, have you got something to drink?'

'There's Coke in the fridge.'

'That'll do.'

I went to get it. As I closed the fridge I couldn't help but feel there was something wrong. That's when I heard the door go.

'Mitch?'

I shoved open the living room door.

'Mitch?'

I stepped in the hall.

'Mitch, you upstairs?'

Then I was back in the living room. My phone was on the table. There was a text. It was from Abi. She was on her way down Bevan. On her way ...

'Oh no.'

My skin crawled. Now I knew why Mitch had called. I ran outside.

'Abi?'

The street was empty. I saw the flash of brake lights at the top of the road.

'Abi!'

My phone rang, drawing me back inside. I clawed for the handset, pressed it to my ear.

'Yes?'

'Hello, Ethan.'

It was Jamie's voice. My blood turned to ice.

'What are you doing with Abi's phone?'

There was a moment's silence then the sound of her voice, thick with terror.

'Ethan!'

I yelled her name. Jamie was back on the line.

'What a touching little scene.'

He waited a beat then told me where to go if I wanted her back.

'Oh, and don't tell me what will happen to me if I touch a hair of her head,' he told me. 'You're not in any position to make threats.'

*

I arrived at the industrial units. It was where the gun had waited for Jamie. I ran all the way, the world lurching as I pounded through the bleak streets. The sweat was turning cold on my skin, sour with fear. The sapphire blue Subaru was parked at the far end of the units. I walked the length of the cracked tarmac road and peered through the window. I recognised Abi's jacket. Horror clutched my throat. Suddenly I cared for somebody else more than I cared about myself.

'Abi?'

The wind was picking up. It rummaged among the litter and rattled the steel shutters. Somewhere a chain clanged.

'Show yourself, Jamie. Tell me what you want.'

The shutters rattled again. This time it wasn't the wind. I spun round and there they were. Dean still had his hand on the shutters. His expression was somewhere between a smirk and a scowl. Jamie had the Walther pistol pressed against Abi's neck just below her ear. Her eyes were startled and afraid, the blush of the single streetlamp on her face.

'Looks like we've got to the endgame, Ethan. Do you remember this piece? It's the one you pulled on me. I had one like it. Remember?'

'I remember.'

'How long is it now?'

'Two years.'

'That long? Doesn't time fly when you're having fun?'

'You've got me now. Let Abi go.'

Jamie grinned. 'Don't be stupid, Ethan. She's a witness. She gets to watch me pop her boyfriend. You can work out the rest.'

'You're sick!'

Jamie shoved Abi roughly into Dean's hands. He marched straight at me and cuffed me to the ground with the Walther, same way I had pistol-whipped him outside the Beehive. The pain was flying glass. It slashed my flesh. My hand was behind my ear. I felt blood. It spilled warm between my fingers and cooled as it fell.

'Where's Mitch?'

'He didn't want to be here,' Jamie answered. 'Isn't that touching? He didn't want to watch. For ever friends, eh? I decided to let him off, you know, for Auld Lang's Syne.'

I knelt on the ground, senses swimming.

'You hit me like that.' He turned the weapon in his hands. 'There's my dried blood on it somewhere.'

I found enough defiance to spit an answer. 'Yes, and I enjoyed getting my own back.'

Jamie drove his boot into my kidneys and I groaned.

'That the best you can do?' Jamie asked. 'I want you to howl. I want you to beg for mercy.' Then he understood. 'Oh, I get it. You're trying to be brave in front of Abi. Isn't that sweet?'

'You want me dead? Why don't you just get on with it, you sick bastard?'

The muzzle pressed against my ear then pulled away again. Jamie strolled round so he was standing in front of me, looking down.

'Maybe this is the wrong way round,' he said. 'Maybe we should make you watch while I smoke the little girlfriend.'

He waved to Dean. Dean dragged Abi towards us.

'Let her go,' I pleaded. 'She hasn't done anything. For God's sake, Jamie. Don't do this.'

Jamie was standing halfway between us.

'Listen to you. You won't beg for your own life, but you'll beg for hers.' He put his hand on his heart and put on a tearful voice. 'That's so ... touching.'

Then he pointed the Walther at Abi's head.

'No!'

The gun roared.

'Abi!' The scream split my head. I was scrambling to my feet. 'Abi!'

The horror was complete. I fell into darkness. That's when I saw Jamie sink to his knees before pitching forward on his face. I saw the stream of scarlet flowing into the weed-choked gutter. For several moments I couldn't make sense of what I was witnessing. Darren was standing over Jamie's lifeless form. Somebody was holding Dean against the shutters of the nearest unit, pressing his face against the dented steel. It was Simmo. Abi was standing just a few metres away. Her face was white with terror, her arms limp by her side. I stumbled forward and wrapped her in an embrace. She was shuddering.

'You're OK. You're OK.'

Simmo got her jacket from the Subaru and dropped it over her shoulders. He spoke in a whisper.

'Get her away from here.'

I nodded.

'Wait for me at the eighteen-step bridge.'

Abi had stopped shivering by the time Simmo arrived. Abi shrank away from him. She kept asking if we should phone 999. I managed to put her off.

'Is she OK?' Simmo asked.

261

'I can speak for myself,' she snapped.

She gave me an unsettling stare. It said she'd heard what happened the night I went after Jamie.

'You're all right then?'

She nodded. 'Is Jamie … ?'

'He's dead.'

'His brother?'

'We let Dean go.'

Abi examined Simmo's features. She didn't recognise him.

'Who are you?'

'My name doesn't matter. You're better not knowing'

'What happened back there?' Abi didn't take her eyes off his face. 'It all happened so fast. I don't understand any of it.'

'This has been coming to Jamie,' Simmo said. 'He started this war when he killed Carl. We've been watching him for a long while.'

'This was planned in advance?'

'You could say that.'

I watched Abi turning his words over in her mind.

'I've got to know something. Does this have anything to do with Ethan?'

Simmo glanced at me. He was good. He answered without any hesitation.

'Outsiders are a complication we don't need. You were in the wrong place at the wrong time.'

Abi seemed to relax a little.

'You've got to listen to me,' Simmo said. 'You got yourselves caught up in something. If you go running to the police, you're never going to be free of it. I can make sure of that.'

Abi protested. 'Somebody was killed!'

It was my turn. 'We can't speak to the police, Abi. You can't say anything to your parents. This is the NSC we're talking about. Neither of us would ever be safe.'

Simmo's voice didn't change. 'Listen to your boyfriend. No police. Stay shtum. You can do that, can't you?'

He explored Abi's face and seemed satisfied with what he saw. I watched him go.

'Who *was* that?' she asked.

'Like he said, you're better not knowing.' I stroked her face. 'You've got to keep this to yourself, Abi. It's important. These people are dangerous.'

'Don't you think I know that?' Her eyes met mine. 'I just saw a man die, killed in cold blood. I won't say anything, Ethan. God knows, I'm terrified of those people. It's a nightmare. I don't want to be involved in any of it.' But there was a rider. 'Something's wrong, Ethan. That was no coincidence.'

'You're wrong,' I told her. 'You heard what he said.'

She drew away. 'You were going to kill Jamie only a few days ago. It wasn't just words, was it? Now this. You're part of a world that makes my flesh creep.'

'This isn't my world,' I told her. 'You heard him. This was between the Tribe and the NSC. We just happened to be in the firing line.'

She reached the top of the steps.

'I want to believe that.'

'Don't go, Abi. Please. Let's talk this through.'

'I don't know if I can believe a word you say. I need time. Don't call me. If I want us to be together, I'll call you.' She started down the steps. 'I want to hear it from your own lips. Did you have anything to do with those people?'

'I followed Jamie, but I couldn't pull the trigger. Tonight was separate, a coincidence. I swear.'

She watched me for a moment then carried on down to the street.

Mum asked about Abi a couple of times. Between the move and preparations for her wedding, she was so busy I managed to fob her off. Alex was a different matter. He knew right away what had happened. But Alex had lived the life. He accepted the law of the jungle. We have never discussed what happened. Maybe we never will. We are brothers. The morning of the wedding he was standing next to me, fighting for a share of the mirror. He knotted his tie.

'Just look at us, bro. We scrub up pretty well.'

We were smart in our suits. Mum was proud of us. Maybe we deserved it. Maybe we didn't.

'When's Abi arriving?'

My neck prickled.

'She's coming straight to the registry office.'

If she was coming at all. I had done as she said. I had stayed away and left her to think things through. The days had passed and I hadn't heard a murmur.

'That right?'

Alex sauntered away to chat to John. I think he enjoyed making me squirm. When we got to the registry office, I saw Eddie and his wife Eileen.

'Looks like you got through it, Ethan,' Eddie said. 'You've got a bright future ahead of you.'

I'd left a space for Abi at the end of the row. Mum glanced round.

'She's cutting it fine.'

'She'll be here,' I said.

By then I had stopped believing it. Could I have done things any other way? Did I have to lose her? The registrar cleared his throat and everybody went quiet.

'Where is she?' Mum whispered.

I shrugged. Then I felt somebody slide in next to me.

'Abi.'

She squeezed my hand.

'It's a good turnout,' she said. She acknowledged the people she knew. 'Hi Alex.'

Mum beamed. 'You look lovely, Abi. Right, we're about to start.'

The ceremony took a matter of minutes. As the next wedding party arrived, we stood around getting our photographs taken on the registry office steps.

'So we're good?'

'I'm here, Ethan. Isn't that enough?'

Her answer gnawed away inside me.

'You do believe me?'

Her eyes narrowed a little then she stroked my hair back the way Mum did when I was little.

'Is there any point talking about this? I've made my decision. We're together. There's nothing more to say.'

'There's a lot more to say.'

'I don't know what I think. Maybe I will never really know what happened at the units. Nobody gets to have everything they want. I suppose it all comes down to two questions. Do I love you? The answer is yes. Can we leave the past behind? I understand survival. Could be you did what you had to do.'

I heard a steeliness in her voice that hadn't been there before.

'We're going to start a new life, Ethan.'

Not a suggestion.

A command.

But even Abi couldn't order things not to have consequences.

I have just got back from town. There's a call from the kitchen.

'Is Abi with you?'

'No, she's gone home.'

My phone buzzes. I see the caller ID and freeze.

'Do you want some tea?'

'What?'

'Some tea.'

'No, it's OK. I've got to go out.'

I am out of the door before Mum can ask any questions. I make the call as I walk down the street.

'Where?'

'Beehive car park.'

Why now? Just when I thought I was home and dry I am walking in the shadow of the past. I start university next month in Manchester. Abi is taking a course at the same campus. We'll be sharing a house in Fallowfield with a couple of lads from Leeds and one of her friends. It isn't much, but you have to start a dream somewhere. Another three weeks and I would have been gone for good. Now this. The cold, fierce night is back to claim me. Darren probably planned it this way. He gave me enough time so I could begin to hope. That way, the taste of despair would be even more bitter. It's a twenty-minute bus ride to the Green. This is the first time I've been back.

I've got a ball of frustration and hopelessness in my throat. My eyes are stinging. This is it. This is how it ends. Darren is finally calling in the debt. I'm in a daze. Simmo is already there as I jog across the waste ground. He's sitting at the wheel of a battered Fiat. Darren wouldn't be seen dead in something like that. I pass the spot where Jamie once knelt before me. To my surprise Simmo is on his own.

'No Darren?'

'I thought he'd be here.'

'You thought wrong.'

There's a snarl in his voice. What the hell is he up to?

'So what do you want?'

'That's no way to talk to an old friend.'

'We're hardly friends.'

I've got his eyes on me, glassy, intense.

'There's plenty of history, Ethan. That time you tried to help me, nobody's ever done anything like that, not once in my life.'

'I didn't do anything.'

'You're the only one who's ever cared.'

It was one little shout. How can that be such a big deal? Somehow, he reminds me of Mitch. They come from the same darkness.

'Do you see anything of Mitch? Peter Mitchell?'

'Didn't you hear? He's the top man in the Tribe these days. He had a straightener with Dean. Your old friend came out on top.' He enjoys watching my surprise. 'Looks like Mitch and me have got unfinished business.

It just goes on, doesn't it? Carl and Jamie. Darren and Jamie. Now me and Mitch. It's what they call symmetry.' The hollow stare is back. 'Back to what I was saying. I owe you for what you did.'

Why all this talk? I just want to know what I'm supposed to do.

'And I owe Darren. Look Simmo, maybe you want to tell me what this is about. I knew there would be a day he would call in the debt.'

For some reason, Simmo's got a smile on his face. 'That day will never come. That's why I wanted to see you.'

He might as well be talking in code.

'I don't understand.'

'You will. Let's just say, I've owed you a debt for some time. Now I've paid it back in full.' He's still finding something really funny. 'In fact, you could say I've paid it back several times over. You're making a new life for yourself. Don't screw it up. You don't want to end up back here. You don't belong anymore. We won't meet again, Ethan.'

He's got his hand out. I frown for a moment, wondering what he's talking about.

'That's it?'

'That's it.'

After some hesitation I shake his hand.

It takes twenty minutes to get home.

'That you, Ethan?'

Alex meets me with the evening paper.

'Look who's made the front page.'

Suddenly the meeting with Simmo makes sense. They found the Rav 4 on the industrial estate, metres from where Jamie was gunned down. Darren was sprawled across the steering wheel. He had a bullet hole in the back of his head. The police think somebody he knew must have pulled the trigger. I find myself nodding.

The gun has done its job.

It's made a weak man strong.

Also by Alan Gibbons

An Act of Love

Seven year old Chris and Imran are sworn blood brothers.

Ten years on they are treading separate paths. The spectre of terrorism has wrecked their friendship. It has changed their lives and could even end them.

A story of two ordinary boys growing up in an extraordinary time, our time. A time of terror, when atrocities don't just happen in TV reports about people in far away places.

Rioting, fighting, maiming and killing are happening here, on our doorstep.

'. . . utterly gripping, honest and courageous . . . We need more books like this.'

www.thebookbag.co.uk

The Defender

When Kenny Kincaid turns his back on the past he has no idea of the legacy he is bequeathing his only son, Ian.

Was he escaping from the paramilitaries, from too much violence and bloodshed, too many victims? Or was he betraying the Cause, turning his back on his comrades-in-arms when he fled clutching his baby son and quarter of a million pounds from a bank job? They think so, and they're intent on revenge. Years later Kenny is still a target - and now so is Ian.

Controversial, compulsive reading, this is an unputdownable thriller.

'A powerful thriller . . . Many layers, no simplifications.'
Irish Times

The Dark Beneath

'Today I shot the girl I love'.

GCSE's are over and sixteen-year-old Imogen is looking forward to a perfect, lazy English summer. But her world is turned upside down by three refugees, all hiding from life. Anthony is fourteen, already an outcast, bullied and shunned by his peers. Farid is an asylum seeker from Afghanistan, who has travelled across continents seeking peace. And Gordon Craig is a bitter, lonely man. She knows all of them, but she doesn't know how dangerous they are. Being part of their lives could cost Imogen her own.

Supercharged with tension and drama, Alan Gibbon's novel is about what happens when the fabric of normality is ripped apart exposing the terrifying dark beneath.

'Turbo-charged with all the same dramatic suspense and explosive concluding events of his previous output this is real lump-in-the-throat stuff, an impassioned outburst written with real feeling and conviction . . . '

School Librarian

F 91B